Whispers of Humility

BOOK SIX IN THE WHISPERS OF NEW ENGLAND SERIES

SUE MILLS

Praise for Whispers of Humility

"Can a stressed-out divorced mother find new love with a somewhat annoying but charming plumber who moonlights doing this or that? Fans of contemporary romance that sprinkles lighthearted elements onto a down-to-earth and sometimes intense approach will enjoy finding out in *Whispers of Humility*."
Virge B., Proofreader, Red Adept Editing

"Norah, a climate change activist in Vermont, is having a hard time meeting the right guy. Shane, a plumber with a complicated past and a cute dog, is used to women falling for his woodsy good looks. When a water-heater crisis leads Shane into Norah's life, she finds him bossy and annoying. He finds her gorgeous but icy. It might just take an environmental disaster for these two to see how perfect they are together." Sarah C., Line Editor, Red Adept Editing

Whispers of Humility

Published by Choose The Front Row Media

Contact: choosethefrontrow@gmail.com

Cover Design by Emily Hensley of smallfrymarketing.com

Editing by Red Adept Editing Services

Proofreading by Mabel Havlin

Paperbock ISBN: 979-8-9986795-3-7

For Dawn Dwyer and Justin Smith
The Lyndon Highway Crew
and
Public Safety Workers
for their tireless efforts to put our town back together

Acknowledgements

This is not a book I was planning to write until Sally Walker planted a seed that was impossible to ignore. I'm grateful to her for the idea and for giving Norah's mother a name.

Sarah C. from Red Adept Editing was my line editor and as always she transformed my words from a manuscript to a novel.

Emily Hensley of Small Fry Marketing created my cover and Shane's tattoo. Her encouragement is invaluable to me.

I'm always grateful to my ARC team for their support and for promoting my books. Can't wait for them to read this one.

This writing career would be nowhere without my husband Gordy, who provides support and encouragement every step of the way. My daughter Katie keeps me humble and reminds me to take a break.

As always, thanks to you my readers for investing some of your precious reading time on my books. I'd love to hear your thoughts on this one. Sally thinks Norah and Shane need a sequel. Tell me if you agree.

Playlist

Adore You – Harry Styles

If the World Was Ending – JP Saxe, Julia Michaels

cardigan – Taylor Swift

What A Time – Julia Michaels, Niall Horan

Vienna – Billy Joel

And I Love You So – Don McLean

See You Again – Wiz Khalifa, Charlie Puth

Need You Now – Lady A

You Turn Me On – Ian Whitcomb

Lover – Taylor Swift

Until I Found You – Stephen Sanchez, Em Beihold9

Contents

1. Christmas Eve   1

2. Tropical Temptations   12

3. New Year's Eve   23

4. Return to Reality   38

5. The Breakup   48

6. A Spa Day   57

7. Revenge   64

8. Tattoos and a Pup   71

9. Leaks Always Happen on Saturday   83

10. Shane's Social Skills Need Work   92

11. No More Tequila   101

12. Norah Finally Hires a Plumber   111

13.	Braids and Boundaries	118
14.	Paddles and Possibilities	128
15.	Past Imperfect	138
16.	Thetford on a Tuesday Night	147
17.	Playing With Passion	157
18.	Connections	168
19.	Longing and Letting Go	180
20.	Meeting Mitzi	189
21.	Shane's Not Invited	200
22.	Writer's Block	213
23.	Swift Water Rescue	224
24.	Shelter From the Storm	233
25.	Picking Up the Pieces	242

Epilogue	257
Afterword	266
Sneak Peak	267
Author's Note	276
Also by	278
About the author	279

"I want to see that tattoo on your back." He slowly turned and shivered as Norah traced the book titles...

Chapter One

Christmas Eve

Norah

"Smile."

This was Norah Taylor's sixth attempt to take a selfie in which both she and her daughter Piper were smiling and had their eyes open. She snapped the picture and glanced at it, with her breath held, knowing that Piper would not stand still for many more.

"Is that one okay? I want to start the movie," Piper whined.

With a grin and a sigh of relief, Norah lowered the phone to show her. "What do you think? Is this a keeper?"

The picture showed mother and daughter smiling widely, dressed in blue plaid leggings and long-sleeved T-shirts emblazoned with the phrase Merry Christmas. Piper was a miniature of Norah except for her cool blue eyes, which matched her father's.

Piper hopped on one foot. "I like it. Send it to Daddy. I want him to see our pajamas!"

Norah found Sam Carpenter in her contacts and added the photo to a message.

Piper says Merry Christmas Eve.

"Okay, that's done. Let's start the movie." Norah found *The Polar Express*, which they always watched on the night before Christmas. She tried to convince Piper to try something else, but she wasn't having it.

"I wish Daddy was here."

I thought he would be until three weeks ago.

Before Norah could say anything, her phone pinged with a message. She swiped the screen to reveal a picture of Sam with his girlfriend, Sophie. They wore red-and-black buffalo-checked pajama pants and black T-shirts trimmed with red. Sam had on a Santa hat, and a black boot encased one of his ankles. He'd been in a construction accident in the fall and had recently transitioned from a cast to the boot.

> *Hey baby girl. Happy Christmas Eve. Have fun with your mom. We can't wait to see you tomorrow.*

Piper crawled into Norah's lap as the movie started. "I miss them."

"I know. But you're going to have an *entire* week with him while I'm gone."

"Do you think they bought pajamas for me so we can all match tomorrow night?"

"Maybe. That'll be a surprise for you," Norah said, and they settled in to watch the movie. When it finished, she carried Piper to her bedroom. "Remember, Santa won't come until you fall asleep."

Norah poured herself a glass of wine then settled on the loveseat. The only light came from the white lights twinkling on the Christmas tree. She needed to put Piper's presents under the tree but wanted a minute to herself first. Sounds were coming from Pip's bedroom. Norah planned to wait until the girl was asleep to play Santa.

The night had gone better than she'd expected. *Thank goodness she didn't throw a fit over Sam not being here. I don't know why he insisted on going up to that cabin tonight when he's going to have to drive back down this way tomorrow.*

3

She shook her head. It wasn't the first time she couldn't understand Sam's actions. *Why do my lady parts still jump when I see him? It's so aggravating that he still affects me that way.* She shook her head again, trying to dislodge her attraction to Sam, which still lingered. *Forty-eight hours from now, I'll be relaxing on a ship in the Caribbean.*

It had been a challenging year. Norah had moved out of the house she shared with Sam a little over a year ago. He was furious and barely said a word to her for weeks. As his anger waned, they started sharing a meal once a week, Piper's stutter eased, and Norah harbored a hope that they would reconcile. Sam had dashed that hope in the spring when he'd told her he wanted more children and wanted to be married. She'd told him she would think about it.

Thank God, Sam was wise enough to know I'd never be happy if I did that. I don't know what I was thinking when I offered. She'd been lonely and tired of taking care of everything by herself on the days she had Piper. And she'd been horny. She still suspected that the reason he wouldn't even touch her last Christmas had something to do with Quinn Michaels. Sam had to have missed their sex life. What a shock it had been to find out he'd been in contact with his first girlfriend.

Norah contemplated her wineglass before she took a sip. She held it in her mouth, savoring the taste and then letting it warm her. Norah had harbored a faint hope that Sam would come back to her, even after he'd made it clear in the spring that they were done, but then he'd invited her to lunch at the beginning of December and squashed that hope when he told her she could have Piper on Christmas Eve. He was going to take Sophie to the cabin he'd been renovating with his brothers and would pick Pip up at noon on Christmas Day.

Sophie Palmer had rented the extra room in Sam's house. They'd dated for a few months, then broken up, and she'd moved out. Sam didn't say what had caused the breakup, but Norah knew he was upset by it. When he was seriously hurt in a construction accident, Sophie volunteered to move back in and take care of him. Norah hadn't known Sam and Sophie had resurrected their relationship, and Sam's news that day at lunch had come as a shock.

It's not like I was sitting around waiting for Sam, but it still hurt. Norah took another swallow of wine and thought about Tom. She'd met him when he joined her agency as a staff lawyer. They didn't work together often, but in the fall, he became involved in a complex snow-making project for a ski area in the southern part of the state. After weeks of back-and-forth, all parties finally came to an agreement. As they wrapped up the details, Norah was thinking about how happy she was to move on to a different project.

"Have dinner with me tomorrow night. To celebrate," Tom blurted.

She expected to meet him at the restaurant, but he insisted on picking her up. They shared an expensive bottle of wine with their meal, and to Norah's surprise, their conversation steered clear of work. Tom revealed he was seven years older than she and had grown up in Connecticut.

"My parents have a second home there. I went to school in New York City, but we spent our summers in Greenwich. You fit the Vermont vibe so well. I figured you'd grown up here," she teased.

"I've been here most of twenty-one years."

Norah cocked her head. "Most of? Did you leave and come back?"

"It's complicated." He grinned. "I got married during my senior year in college." He refilled his wineglass. "She was pregnant, and we were in love. It seemed like the right thing to do. Law school had accepted me, and she had one year left of grad school. Neither of us wanted to abandon those dreams, so we struggled through that first year. She finished even with a newborn. We knew we wanted to settle near her parents, so when she got a job offer here, she moved home while I stayed in Connecticut. We had a long-distance relationship until I finished law school. My feet were in both states for a couple of years."

"That must have been rough." She cocked her head again. "You *are* divorced, right?"

Tom leaned back. "Yes. I was married for fifteen years and have been divorced for six. Our son will turn twenty-one in January." He shrugged. "The relationship ran out of gas, if

6

you're wondering. There wasn't any egregious behavior. We're still friends."

"That's what happened with my ex and me. We were only together for eight years, though." *That's mostly true.*

Norah was more relaxed at dinner than she'd been in years, and when Tom walked her to the door of her little cottage, the kiss that he leaned in for did not surprise her. She invited him in, and they made their way to her bedroom. Their relationship had grown from there, although in many ways, Norah was holding him at arm's length. Pip had met him only a couple of times, and Norah didn't allow him to stay over on nights when she had her daughter. He had proposed a cruise for the period between Christmas and New Year's, and with a little cajoling, Norah had agreed. Sam was ecstatic about having Piper for an entire week, and Norah was looking forward to a change of pace.

Piper's room was quiet, and Norah tiptoed back to make sure she was asleep. Pip clutched a purple unicorn, and Norah smiled as she listened to her even breathing. Piper loved to talk, and Norah felt like the only time the house was silent was when the girl was asleep. Despite her love for her daughter, the constant chatter overwhelmed her, and she was often exhausted at day's end.

There was a soft knock on the door while Norah was arranging the presents. She opened it to find Tom leaning on the doorjamb. He smiled warmly. "I'm on my way home from Rachel's and wanted to see you. Hope you don't mind."

Rachel was a coworker who always had a party on Christmas Eve. Everyone raved about it when they returned to work after the holiday, but Norah had never attended.

Next year, Sam can have Piper on Christmas Eve, and I'll go to Rachel's party. How much fun will it be to dress up and enjoy adult company?

Reaching for Tom's hand, she whispered, "Come on in. We must be quiet. I don't want Pip to wake up. And I need to go to bed soon. She'll be up before sunrise."

Tom glanced at her empty wineglass. "Will you have another one with me?" When Norah nodded, he walked to the kitchen for a glass and the bottle. He filled the glasses then gathered her into his arms. "Love the pajamas."

Norah blushed. She had forgotten what she was wearing. "Flannel is all the rage. Sorry you didn't get the memo." Tom was wearing a white shirt, a red tie, and black pants. "Let's sit." As they sank onto the loveseat, Tom reached up to loosen his tie.

Norah eyed him warily. "You can't stay tonight."

"Just getting comfortable." He brought his lips to hers, starting softly as he always did and then becoming more insistent. His kisses were long and lingering, and Norah's favorite part of sex with him. His hands traveled up and down her back. "Maybe you should add flannel to your everyday wardrobe. I could learn to like this." He brought her hand to the bulge in his pants, and she stroked him softly. A whispered moan escaped his lips as he thrust against her. "This won't end in the bedroom, will it?"

"No." Norah had made the rules very clear. He couldn't stay over when Piper was with her.

One of her hands continued to stroke him, and the other moved his hand to her breast. The feel of his fingers through the flannel was electric, and her body tingled in response. They continued teasing each other until Norah noticed the time.

"It's almost eleven. She'll probably be awake at five. And tomorrow is going to be a long day. I need to go to sleep."

Tom reluctantly stood. "I can't wait to have the entire week with you." He adjusted himself. "This erection is probably going to last until we get to Miami."

Norah sank into another of his kisses before he walked to the door. "We're meeting Sam at noon. He and Sophie drove all the way up to that cabin for one night when they have to meet me tomorrow, and then they're going to turn around and drive back up there to celebrate with his family. Does it make any sense to you?" She couldn't hide her aggravation.

Tom wrapped his arms around her and held her tightly, ensuring that she could feel his erection. "That's his problem, not yours."

"But it *is* mine! Because now I must drive fifteen miles north to meet him at a highway rest stop. Exchanging our daughter is going to feel like a clandestine drug deal. If he'd stayed home, he could have come over tonight. Piper missed him! And tomorrow morning, I could have been at his house in less than ten minutes."

Tom silenced her with another kiss. "Are you sure it was Piper who missed him?"

Norah stepped back. "What are you implying? I didn't care if he came by. It's been more than a year, Tom. I'm well over him."

He held her in his gaze for several seconds then pulled her back to him. "I wasn't implying anything. I don't want to talk about Sam Carpenter tonight or at any point in the next ten days." His fingers tangled in her hair as he fluttered kisses around her ear, then down her neck. He moved his hand from her hair and fondled her breast through the flannel again. "I'm not kidding about this material. It's hot as hell."

Norah sighed and pressed closer. She considered changing her stance and leading him to her bedroom. Piper seldom woke up once she was asleep. She'd never know. The fire between Norah's legs grew as Tom continued to tease her nipple then brought his mouth back to hers for more of the kisses that weakened her resolve.

But I know how it will end. She broke away. "I have to go to bed." She punctuated her words with a brief kiss. "I'll see you tomorrow."

After several more kisses, Tom finally stepped away. He ran his hand over her hair. "Till the morning."

After he left, Norah locked the door. She stopped for one last look at Piper before going to her bedroom. She paused, still aroused, then closed the door and flipped the lock. She shoved her leggings to the floor, yanked on the drawer in her nightstand, and reached way to the back. Lying on her bed, Norah stroked her breast then pinched the nipple, remembering the feel of Tom's touch. She switched on the vibrator, brought it to her clit, and moaned softly as the waves of her orgasm overtook her.

When they stopped, she tossed her head back against the pillow, heaving a deep sigh. She gazed at the ceiling. The best part of sex with Tom was the foreplay. His kisses and touches set her on fire but had never resulted in an orgasm when they had intercourse. The passion he stirred faded as soon as he buried his cock in her. She'd become adept at faking, and she was sure Tom was unaware of how unsatisfied he left her. *Thank God for vibrators.*

Chapter Two

Tropical Temptations

Norah

"Mommy, when are they going to get here?" Piper was bouncing impatiently in her booster seat. "Do you think they forgot?"

"No, sweetie. We got here a few minutes early. Your dad texted that they're on their way."

She tamped down the aggravation overtaking her. *We agreed to meet at noon, and it's five of. We are early.* In the year since they'd split, Sam had never been late picking up Piper. Norah needed to remember that.

Tom reached over from the passenger seat and placed his hand on her arm. "Is that them?"

He'd arrived at Norah's an hour earlier, with a present for Piper. She had ripped the paper off eagerly and was delighted to find a set of horses that would fill the stable Santa had brought her. After Norah deftly convinced her that the horses and stable would be fine while she was with her father, the three of them bundled into the car. After dropping off Piper, Tom and Norah would drive to Norah's family in Connecticut to celebrate Christmas and fly to Miami the next morning.

The approaching car had barely stopped when Piper was streaking across the parking lot. Sam stepped out of the passenger's side and braced for her approach, which was always the same.

"Daddy!" She threw herself at him, and he swooped her into his arms. "Did you ask her?" Her whispered question was loud enough for Norah to hear from where she waited with Tom.

"I sure did."

"And I said yes." The pretty redhead who'd been driving got out of the car and walked over to join their hug.

Piper struggled to be put down. "Let me see the ring!"

Sophie extended her left hand, a simple one-carat diamond solitaire twinkled on her finger.

"Ohhh," Piper whispered. "It's beautiful." She turned to look at her mother. "Daddy and Sophie are getting married. He asked her last night." She hopped on one foot. "And I kept it a secret! I told you I would, Daddy." Her eyes sparkled.

Married. Norah flushed and swallowed hard before trying to get words out. "Congratulations." She grinned at Piper and then looked back at Sam. "I can't believe she didn't tell me."

"Me either. And she's known for over a week."

Tom extended his hand to Sam. "Congratulations. That must have been an epic Christmas Eve."

"It was." There was an awkward silence. "We should get going, baby girl. Your mom has a lot longer drive than we do." Sam looked toward Norah. "I'd get her bags, but I'm still restricted with this boot."

Sophie stepped toward Norah's car. "I'll get them. Sorry, I spaced out for a minute."

Tom raised his hand. "Leave it to me." He smiled at Sophie. "You must have well-deserved engagement brain fog." When they were back on the road, he asked, "Are you surprised about their engagement?"

"No," Norah lied. She shook her head. "Maybe a little by the timing. He's only known her for a year. They became a couple in May and then broke up during the summer. So it seems a little fast." She sighed. "I bet Sophie's biological clock is a factor. I'm happy for them." It was a slight white lie.

Tom stroked her arm. "Piper seems excited."

"She loves Sophie. The bigger surprise is her keeping it a secret. She usually spills everything she knows."

14

"Is it hard for you to leave her? She could have come with us on the cruise."

"Sam would never agree to that," Norah said, though she wasn't sure. She and Piper had spent a week in Maine during the summer, with no argument from Sam. After the initial acrimony over how Piper would split her time between them, they now came easily to an agreement anytime one of them wanted to bend the custody rules. Norah was looking forward to having no responsibility. "They're going to Rhode Island to visit Sophie's family. She has two teenage sisters, twins, as a matter of fact, and Pip has fallen in love with them. Whenever she spends time with them, she comes back to me and it's 'Des this' and 'Gracie that.' They're the sisters she longs for."

They were silent for several minutes.

Then Norah continued. "She'll have a great time this week. Plus, Sam's brother Joe is getting married on New Year's Eve. Pip would not have missed that."

Four hours later, Norah pushed the code to open the gate to her parents' estate. She was nervous about introducing Tom to her mother. She didn't give a flying fig what her father thought, but she knew her mother would latch onto Tom like a barnacle on a boat. Mitzi Taylor had accepted Sam, primarily because he'd fathered her granddaughter, but never failed to let Norah

15

know she expected a better partner for her than a man from rural Vermont who always wore a flannel shirt and jeans when he visited.

Norah snuck a glance at Tom. He was wearing khaki pants, a white open-collared shirt, and a black sweater that she suspected was cashmere. *Oh yeah, Mom is going to fall in love with him.* She took a deep breath. *And then she'll have grand expectations as to where the relationship is going.*

By the time they approached the front door, Norah's mother was waiting to greet them. Norah embraced her lightly, kissing her cheek. "Mother, this is Tom Sindal. Tom, my mother, Mitzi Taylor."

Tom leaned in to kiss her cheek. "It's nice to meet you. I can see where Norah got her beauty." He handed her a decorative wine bag. "Norah said you're a fan of white wine."

Oh God. I should have known how charming he would be. She smiled at her mother's look of approval. "Where's everyone else?"

"In the great room. We'll eat in half an hour."

Norah's family had stopped exchanging gifts among the adults years earlier, but Norah had brought gifts for her niece and nephews. While the children unwrapped their presents, Norah introduced Tom to her father and siblings.

They moved to the dining room, and Mitzi questioned Tom. "Where are you from?"

"I grew up in Darien. My dad was the president of Darien Savings. He and my mother moved to Arizona a few years ago. My sister is an artist and lives in New Mexico. It's nice to be included in a family dinner."

"Where did you go to college?"

"I went to Yale."

Norah felt the sidelong glance from her mother.

Mitzi continued the questions. "How did you end up in Vermont? We know Norah went there because she appreciated their progressive environmental positions."

Norah's father interrupted before Tom could respond. "Frankly, we think it's time for her to find another state to save. Her degree from Columbia is being wasted in that backwater. She could have a tremendous impact here or in New York. It's time for her to give up her little social experiment."

Norah's face grew hot. This was not a new topic with her father, but she'd hoped he would have enough grace not to bring it up with someone he'd just met, and at a holiday dinner. *I should have known better.*

Her father wasn't done. "When she left the Agency of Natural Resources, we thought surely she'd be done with Vermont. It was rather humiliating the way they let her go. Instead, she let them move her to a brand-new agency. A demotion in everyone's eyes, I'm sure."

"It was a lateral move, Father." Norah spoke through gritted teeth.

17

"Norah's doing great things in Vermont. She'd be sorely missed—by the agency and by me." Tom's voice was even and firm. "My ex-wife is from Vermont. We were young when our son was born, and living near her parents enabled us to both pursue our career goals. I fell in love with the state. I'll never leave."

Norah relished watching her father back off. She especially liked Tom's mention of his ex-wife's career goals. She was glad he didn't act like his job was the most important one. *How long do we have to stay before leaving for the airport hotel? Booking that early-morning flight was the smartest thing I ever did.*

Two hours later, they were on their way to Hartford. "Your family doesn't like you living in Vermont?" Tom asked.

"No." Norah sighed. "It was all right when I took the job after graduation, because it was a prestigious position. They thought I'd stay a few years, gain some experience, and then leave. Honestly, that was my five-year plan. But..." She sighed again. "By the time I got to five years, I'd met Sam, and we were expecting Piper. It didn't seem like the right time to be looking for a job and making a move. And then... I just stayed."

"Did you and Sam ever talk about moving? Would he have left?"

"We never talked about it. I knew there would be promotions coming, and I didn't want to look for a different job when I was six months pregnant. Our life worked until it didn't. Let's talk about something else."

"You never really told me why you left Natural Resources. Your father made it sound like something nefarious happened."

"We didn't agree on strategy. I wanted the agency to take a stronger stance on climate offenders than they were willing to do. We agreed to part ways, and I went to work with the Climate Initiatives office, which is a better fit."

I could kill my father. I hope Tom doesn't ask any more questions.

The next afternoon, they stood on the deck, watching the harbor fade into the distance. Tom tapped his flute of champagne against Norah's. She'd changed into a flowy green sundress, and Tom was wearing khaki shorts with a black T-shirt. A server took their flutes, and Tom's now-empty hand went around her waist.

He sniffed her hair. "Did you change to a coconut scent because we're in the tropics?" He feathered kisses down her neck to her bare shoulder. "I could learn to like this summer wardrobe."

She shuddered in response to his kisses. "The lotion in our stateroom is coconut." She leaned against him, his closeness turning her on in the same way it always did.

A server walked by, carrying a tray of champagne glasses, and Tom snagged two of them. "Let's enjoy these on our balcony."

Back on the balcony, he sank onto the chaise lounge, pulling Norah down between his legs. The air was warm, and they watched the sun paint the sky a dozen shades of pink. Darkness washed over them, and Tom moved Norah's hair out of the way so he could nibble on her neck. He slid one strap of her dress down over her shoulder and let his hand wander to her breast. He cradled it, rubbing his thumb over the nub, and Norah's heartbeat quickened. His kisses moved from her hairline down her neck and onto her back. Tom never rushed anything, and Norah had learned to enjoy his tender worship of her body. His erection was obvious as she relaxed against him. Their balcony was completely private from prying eyes, but she could hear the guests in the staterooms on both sides of theirs.

Tom slipped the other strap off and stroked Norah's skin. "Is it that coconut lotion making your skin so soft?"

Norah moaned. *Maybe having sex out here will tip the balance. The warm night air, the illicitness of almost being out in public...* Her mind drifted to the first hike she and Sam had taken and how they'd made love in a secluded glen near the summit. They'd both experienced explosive orgasms that had moved their relationship from casual dating to something more. Tom's hand moved between her legs, and his teasing brought her back to the balcony. Another moan escaped her lips.

"Shh, shh. No one will even know we're out here if we're quiet," he said. One hand continued to caress her center lazily while the other circled her nipple.

Even though Norah knew what was coming, her body lurched when he finally pinched the nub. She shifted her position so her lips could reach his. They moved hungrily together. Her hand found the bulge in his pants, and he moaned softly as she applied pressure.

"Now, who needs to be quiet?" Eventually, the balconies adjoining theirs became silent. "Think they've gone to dinner?" Norah whispered.

"Maybe. We've got time to finish this before our dining time."

Norah responded by unzipping his shorts and burrowing her fingers into his boxers. He thrust against her and then seamlessly stood and led her into the stateroom. Her dress was in a puddle on the balcony. Tom hooked his finger into her thong and slid it to the floor, before shoving his shorts and boxers off. They'd discussed birth control before their first time in bed, with Norah assuring Tom that she had it covered. They'd used a condom that first night in her cottage and then both got tested to ensure that they were clean.

Norah reached for the hem of Tom's shirt and pulled it over his head. She put her arms around him, savoring the skin-to-skin contact. He was taller and leaner than Sam, and Norah liked the way they fit together, with his erection between her legs. They edged closer to the bed, and Tom gently lowered her to the mattress then plunged into her heat. His breathing quickened, and Norah could feel his climax approaching. She moaned, and her pelvis rose to meet his thrusts. He came with the groan she'd heard dozens of times before, and she let loose with the fake orgasm she had perfected over the past few months.

Tom rolled to the side but kept her clasped in his arms. He sprinkled kisses then murmured, "This is going to be a great trip."

Norah's stomach growled while they were still entwined. "I need to shower before dinner." She disentangled herself, walked out to the deck to retrieve her dress, and entered the bathroom.

Dammit. Would it have been better if we'd stayed on the balcony? Or how about if I were on top for a change? They'd never had sex in any other position than missionary. *He's perfect in every way except that I can't come with him.*

Chapter Three

New Year's Eve

Norah

AFTER A STOP IN Nassau that included a sunset dinner cruise, the ship proceeded to Tortola. In the morning, Norah and Tom boarded a ferry for the sail to the baths at Virgin Gorda.

"I've been here before," Tom said as the boat docked. "We don't need to take the tour. Let's explore on our own."

When they arrived at the Baths, Norah removed her cover-up, revealing a light-blue bikini. Tom's eyes raked over her before he stuffed the coverup into the bag with the snorkeling gear.

"Let's explore before lunch then hike over to Devil's Bay. We can snorkel there." He led her into crystal-clear water cluttered with enormous boulders.

Norah sank into the turquoise water and basked in its warmth. "I feel very insignificant next to these boulders." She sighed. "I think a winter vacation like this might have to happen every year."

"It's a pleasant break. I grew up coming here with my family every April. Let me show you more."

At lunchtime, he led her to a beach shack. They shared a salad made with river shrimp. At the end of the meal, the server brought out two shot glasses of rum.

"It's an island tradition." Tom tapped his glass against Norah's. "To beach days. Ready to go to Devil's Bay? It'll be less crowded."

They snorkeled, and the colorful fish awed Norah. "These are beautiful. I told myself I wouldn't do this..." She grinned at Tom. "Piper would love this. But I don't want to spend our whole vacation bemoaning the fact that she isn't with us."

"It's understandable. Let's lie on the beach."

Norah and Tom found a secluded spot and baked in the sun. Norah dozed. When she awoke, she told Tom she was going to cool off in the water.

Tom stayed on shore, and Norah could feel his eyes watching her before he lay back on the towel. The beach was almost empty, and she was the only one in the water. She walked farther away from land than she had when Tom was with her then flipped onto her back. The salty water increased her buoyancy, and it took little effort for her to stay afloat. The blue of the sky hypnotized her, and she lost track of time. When she flipped upright, she was shocked to find the bottom had fallen away. Treading water, she pivoted back toward land, realizing she was farther from shore than she'd intended to go. She turned onto her stomach and began paddling. After several minutes, she raised her head and saw that she'd made no progress. She paddled again, only to find the same result when she took a break. She was still far from shore, maybe even farther than when she'd started. And she was getting tired.

Riptide? I know what to do, but in all my time swimming in the Atlantic, I never had to. She looked at the shore again, where Tom was still prone on the sand and everyone else had left. *Should I call for help? God, no. I'll sound pathetic.* Taking a couple of deep breaths, she reminded herself not to panic. *If I swim parallel to shore, I'll move out of the current. I can do this.*

Norah swam steadily for several minutes, not making any progress. The current's pull had not waned. Tears began to fill her eyes. *I'm going to drown out here. I'm never going to see Piper again. She's going to be motherless.*

Stop. She started swimming again and, after a few minutes, felt the current ease. She shifted direction and began swimming toward the beach.

"I've got you, babe. Don't fight me." Suddenly, Tom's arms were around her. "Relax. Let me do the work."

She struggled away from him. "I'm fine." In what seemed like no time, she saw him stand, and after a few more strokes, she could touch the sandy bottom.

"Can you walk? I'll help you." His voice was soft, but his arms were strong, supporting her.

Norah was trembling, but she didn't like Tom acting like she was incapable of standing on her own feet. "I'm fine," she said again.

"I shouldn't have let you go out by yourself. Or I shouldn't have fallen asleep. I'd never forgive myself if something happened to you."

Oh my God. I feel like the helpless little woman.

The next day, they docked in Antigua, where they were to go out with Eco Boat Tours and do more snorkeling. Tom ordered breakfast to be delivered to their balcony.

As they ate, Norah said, "I don't think I can go in the water." The close call still spooked her. She'd insisted that no one be told what had happened. Tom wanted her to be checked by the medical personnel, but she refused. "I'm embarrassed. I was so stupid."

"It could have happened to anyone. Do you want to skip the eco tour? We can spend the day on the ship."

"No, this is the excursion I've been looking forward to the most. I want to see the island's ecosystem. It's supposed to be extraordinary. You can snorkel, I'll stay on the boat."

That night, as they watched the sunset from the balcony, Tom said, "I did not like leaving you on that boat."

"Why? I was fine. Talking to the crew was fascinating."

"I figured you would be, but it still didn't feel right." He took her hands and spun her to face him. "You must go in the water tomorrow. You told me how much you and Piper enjoy visiting the Maine coast. I don't want yesterday's experience to ruin that for you. The longer you wait, the harder it will be."

"Kinda like getting back on the horse that threw me?"

"Yes. I'll be right by your side, and it doesn't have to be for long. But you must do it."

Norah knew he was right, and that night, she dreamed about floating on the water. The next day, as they disembarked on the cruise line's private island, Norah said, "Let's do it now. I want to get it over with so I can relax when we have our massages later."

With snorkel gear firmly in place, they backed into the water. As soon as it was deep enough, Tom turned her around. "Come on. You can do this."

He guided the snorkel into her mouth and held her hand as she sank into the water. She clutched his hand as they glided near the bottom, seeing mostly parrotfish and angelfish. Norah relaxed and eased her grip on Tom's hand. Just before the two of them turned back, a school of surgeonfish surrounded them. The blue haze delighted Norah, and she raised her free hand, letting Tom know she wanted to stop.

When the fish moved on, they headed toward the shore, where Tom removed the snorkel from her mouth and pushed her mask to the top of her head. "How are you doing?"

"That was amazing. Thank you for pushing me." She bent to take off the flippers. "I must bring Piper here. She'd love it." Norah rolled her eyes. "I know I said I wouldn't keep bringing her up."

He kissed her lips. "She's your child and is never out of your mind. I know how that is." He picked up the masks and flippers. "Let's get some lunch and then enjoy our massages."

There was a bonfire on the beach before the tenders arrived to transport everyone back to the ship. Norah and Tom sat in a secluded corner, away from the crowd of families with children.

He leaned over to whisper in her ear. "Do you want a s'more? I can risk the onslaught to roast a marshmallow."

Norah smiled. "I'm fine with this." She raised the shot glass a server had handed her a few minutes earlier. "I like this rum habit."

The rum wasn't the only thing Norah liked. Their day had been nearly perfect. She appreciated Tom's insistence that she get back in the water but had mixed feelings about holding his hand. It had given her the strength to move forward, knowing she wouldn't be alone. But she didn't like it. *When have I ever let myself lean on a man?*

That had never been a factor with Sam. She was the older, more established one. Her job paid more, and she had an advanced degree from an Ivy League college. Norah had not depended on Sam for anything, and she expected that to continue in any future relationship. She would never be dependent on a man.

Would I have gotten back in without Tom? Yes. Maybe not as quickly, but I wouldn't have let the incident keep me out of the water.

The massages on the beach had been heavenly, making the day even more perfect. The tables had been side by side on a secluded part of the island. Steel drum music played faintly in the background, and any residual tension was gone by the time the masseuse finished. They'd spent the rest of the day in beach chairs.

Tom was as relaxed as she was, and she realized that while he was strong and steady, he didn't have a constant desire to be in motion. She didn't think he would try to dominate her. Maybe this could work. She grasped his hand and lost herself in the flames.

29

"Have you ever considered giving Piper that sister you said she wants?" he asked.

"What?" His words jerked Norah out of her mellow mood.

"You said Pip wants a sister. I'd be happy to help you with that."

"Are you...?" Norah shook her head. *Is he saying he wants to have a child with me? Maybe the rum has addled my brain. Or his.*

Before she could voice her thoughts, Tom spoke again. "You're an extraordinary woman. I'd love to have a child with you."

"Your son is almost twenty-one years old. You'd start over again?" *What am I doing? Why am I even engaging in this conversation? Another child is not in my future.*

"I've always known I'd take a second chance on fatherhood if the right woman came along. You could be that woman. I want to take what's going on between us to the next level."

Norah was at a loss for words. Sam had told her plenty of times how icy her tone could be, and she didn't want to come across that way with Tom. Having another child was the last thing she planned on doing. But there was no way she could say that without sounding like a total bitch.

As her silence stretched, Tom finally said, "Let's catch the early tender so we avoid the crowd."

Back in their stateroom, he peeled off her coverup and untied her bikini top then hooked his fingers into the bottom and shoved it to the floor. Norah stood silent as he ran his hands up and down her sides and caressed her waist. He moved to fondle her breast as he kissed her.

Norah fought the arousal that always came from his touch, but her body wasn't getting the message from her mind. A moan escaped her lips, and Tom lowered her to the bed. His fingers caressed her clit and slid in easily. He replaced his fingers with his cock, and Norah's glimmer of an orgasm faded to nothingness. He stroked faster, and Norah, for the first time, did not pretend. After he came, she rolled away and stared into the darkness, feeling the motion of the ship slicing through the waves as she tried to sort out her feelings.

When she awoke, Tom was on the balcony, watching the sunrise. It was New Year's Eve, their last day at sea. Norah pulled on shorts and a tank top before joining him. The silence was as thick as it had been the night before.

Tom turned and kissed her cheek. "Let's get some breakfast."

They sat with a couple who had been with them on the sunset cruise in the Bahamas. The four of them discussed the excursions they'd done, and the men decided to play mini golf on the top deck.

"I'm going to the adult pool with my book. I've only read two chapters, and I plan to finish it before the end of the cruise." Norah hoped her declaration made it clear that she wanted the day to herself.

She had a blessed day alone until Tom appeared late in the afternoon. He cocked his head, silently asking for permission to sit next to her. Norah nodded, and he sank onto the lounger.

"How was mini golf?" she asked.

Norah had spent the day trying to figure out what to say to him and finally decided she couldn't touch the subject of children, or even their relationship, until they were home. She would stick to inconsequential topics and sort out the rest later. Which was not like her—she faced everything head-on.

"It was fun. We played three games. He won two. Then we went to the casino. I won five hundred dollars playing blackjack."

"Awesome!" Norah managed to conjure genuine enthusiasm for his win.

"How's the book coming?"

"Good. I have a hundred pages left, so I'll finish it on the flight tomorrow."

"Look..." Tom rubbed the back of his neck. "We don't have to go to that dinner tonight." The ship was having an extra formal night to celebrate the holiday. "We can go to the buffet instead."

"I want to go." She paused. "Unless you don't want to. I've been looking forward to dressing up."

"Okay, then we should. We've got some time. I'm going swimming."

Norah watched him and considered joining him. Twenty-four hours earlier, she would have been at his side. But now—she couldn't. "I'm going back to the room. I want to take a shower."

With half an hour left until the new year, they made their way back to the stateroom. There would be fireworks at midnight, and they had agreed, early in the week, that they would watch them from the privacy of their balcony. The meal had been extraordinary—five courses, each paired with a bottle of wine. They started with lobster bisque shooters then moved to seared scallops with a citrus-and-fennel salad. A seafood platter, featuring oysters on the half shell and Alaskan king crab legs, preceded the decadent main course of beef wellington. The tenderloin, cooked to a perfect medium rare, was enveloped in mushroom duxelles and encased in a delicate puff pastry. Truffle mashed potatoes accompanied the beef. A raspberry-and-white-chocolate mousse capped the meal. The wine had eased the tension between them, and they'd laughed easily throughout the evening.

Tom carried a bottle of champagne, and Norah had the flutes someone had given them as they left the dining room. "That's one of the best meals I've ever had," Norah murmured.

"It was superb," Tom agreed. "Are we going to stay dressed up?" Norah was wearing a beaded red gown, and Tom had on a tuxedo with a red tie.

"Let's change." Norah giggled. "I want to be comfortable." She slipped out of her dress and pulled on a tank top and shorts before moving to the balcony.

Tom joined her, popping the top on the champagne bottle and filling the flutes before he sat down. He touched his flute to hers. "To the new year. And new relationships." They drained the glasses, and Tom refilled them. "About last night..."

No! Norah's mind screamed. *Don't spoil the night by bringing that up again.*

"I'm sorry I left you behind."

Oh my God. He's talking about me not coming. Little does he know...

She tittered. "No big deal."

"I think it was. I don't like to be that inconsiderate, and I know by the way you acted this morning that it bothered you."

Norah moved to his lap. "Make it up to me." She brought her lips to his, wanting the long, sensuous kisses she'd learned to expect from him.

Tom buried his fingers in her hair as his lips moved under hers. His tongue nudged her mouth, and she welcomed him in. He explored, slowly, gently, and she could taste the champagne. His kisses and the wine washed away all thoughts of the night before.

I didn't think kissing him could get any better, but this alcohol-fueled buzz is moving it to another level.

She broke away from the kiss. "We need more champagne." She stood and stumbled as she took a step toward the table where the flutes sat.

"Whoa, careful." Tom jumped up to steady her.

Norah stroked his cheek. Then with a devilish grin, she pulled off her tank top and grabbed his T-shirt. "This has to go." She filled the flutes, and when she turned back to Tom, he still had his shirt on. She tilted her head and ran her hand up and down his chest. "Come on," she teased.

"You're a little drunk."

Laughter burst forth. "More than a little."

"I won't do something you're going to regret tomorrow."

"The thing I'm going to regret is you not taking off that shirt." When he continued to hesitate, Norah sighed. "I'm not so drunk that I don't know what I'm doing. Stop being such a gentleman." As she brought the flute to her mouth, some champagne splashed onto her breast. After swallowing a mouthful, she looked at him with a challenge in her eyes. "I need a towel... or a tongue."

Tom leaned toward her, and his tongue snaked out, lapping the valley where the liquid had settled.

Norah shivered. "Yesss." She reached for his shirt and yanked it off.

"If you're sure..."

"I'm sure." Norah wrapped her arms around him. "Kiss me more. I love your kisses. I live for your kisses."

Norah pushed him onto the chaise. Their kisses were a long exploration that started softly and ramped up to passion that left them lunging toward each other while fireworks lit up the sky. Unconcerned about being quiet, she moaned as Tom stroked her back and moved his mouth to her breasts. He teased her, leisurely tracing circles around the nipple.

As the fireworks faded, Tom whispered, "Let's take this inside." He tried to lift her off his lap.

"No. Here." She stood, shoved her shorts to the floor, then grasped his hand and pulled him up.

She stared at him as he slowly unbuttoned his shorts and pushed them to the floor. His cock sprang free, and Norah grasped it, bringing forth a groan. She stroked from tip to balls, teasing him as he'd done to her. He placed his hand over hers, increasing the speed and the pressure. His breathing quickened.

"Not sure where this is going." He moved his hand between her legs. His fingers rubbed her clit then plunged into her.

"Right here," Norah moaned. "We're going right here." He pushed her toward the chaise. "No." She danced around him. "You sit."

She watched as he warily sat down. She gazed at him, taking in the glory of his body—lean but with chiseled abs and muscular thighs. His eyes traveled up and down, drinking her in. She reached for the champagne bottle and emptied the last of it into their glasses. Still standing, she tapped her flute to his in one final toast then straddled him, his cock fitting perfectly between her legs.

He thrust upward, and she backed away. "Not yet."

"Tell me what you want."

"Kisses. I want those incredible kisses. And your hands all over my body and your mouth on my breasts. I want to hold your cock and feel it getting harder. Then I want you to hammer it into me. I want you to show me I drive you out of your mind with desire. Because that's what you do to me."

Long kisses gave way to Tom's mouth nipping at her nubs. Norah rubbed her center on his cock then took it in her hand. It was rock-hard. She stroked quickly, letting her desire flow through her fingertips. Finally, feeling like she was going to explode, she guided him in. He filled her completely, more than he had before. She stilled, wanting to achieve the orgasm she'd been craving but not wanting to risk falling short again.

Tom shifted on the lounger, trying to reach her lips. When he did, she couldn't remain still. She tried to keep it slow until his hand snaked between them, and he pinched her nipple. It felt like he'd lit a rocket, and she moved on him, not caring if her pursuit of climax matched the faking she'd done. The waves started, and she orgasmed with a low groan. She continued to slide his cock in and out, savoring the sensations until she was sated and collapsed against him. Lost in her bliss, she had no idea if he'd come and frankly didn't care.

Chapter Four

Return to Reality

Norah

PERSISTENT POUNDING AWOKE NORAH the next morning. Prying her eyes open, she realized the noise was in her head. She groaned and closed her eyes.

"Norah." Tom tapped her arm. "Sit up and take this."

She opened one eye and saw him standing at the bedside, holding a glass of water and two Tylenol. She struggled to a sitting position, looking at him with her one open eye. Closing it and opening the other, she reached for the glass. "What time is it?"

"Eight." They were to disembark at eleven. "We have time for breakfast. Do you want me to pack for you?"

With difficulty, she got to her feet, tucking the blanket around her. "You don't need to pack for me. I want to shower first." Her feet tangled in the blanket, and she stumbled, reaching for the bed.

Tom caught her. "I've got you."

Norah hiked the blanket up and stepped out of his arms. On her way to the shower, she muttered, "How are you so perky?"

Gradually, with the steaming water pounding over her, she began to feel human. *I told him I would not regret anything, and I don't. Except perhaps I should have drunk a little less wine.*

His words from two days ago came rushing back. "You're an extraordinary woman. I'd love to have a child with you." *He's going to think that wild abandon last night means I'm on the same page he is. I don't know what page I'm on, but there aren't any children in that book.*

"What time will Sam bring Piper home?" Tom asked.

It was late afternoon on New Year's Day, and they were nearly back at Norah's house. The day had been long, with the two of them shuttling from the ship to the airport, flying home, and now making the drive back to Vermont. Her hangover hadn't helped, and she had slept for most of the flight. Conversation was strained between her and Tom, with no mention of the wild sex on the balcony.

"I texted Sam when we left Hartford, so I expect them soon," she said.

"You must have missed her."

"Of course."

"We should book another cruise and bring her with us. How about April vacation?"

Norah's stomach sank. "I can't make plans like that without consulting Sam."

"Okay. Talk to him, and then we can make plans next week."

Norah turned into her driveway, and Sam's car pulled in behind her. Piper popped out of the back seat and ran to Norah.

"Mommy!" She threw herself into Norah's arms. "I missed you!"

Norah hugged her tightly. "Oh, I missed you, too, baby girl." To her surprise, tears flooded her eyes.

Sam and Sophie stood near their car. "Sorry to not even give you a chance to unpack your suitcases. She couldn't wait to see you," he said.

"Sophie, show Mommy the picture from Uncle Joe's wedding. I had the *prettiest* dress."

"Still no driving?" Norah asked Sam while Sophie was searching for the right photo.

Sam shook his head. "I think I'm ready, but the doctor said not until I've done a couple more physical therapy sessions.

40

After twelve weeks of staying off that foot, I will not do anything to mess it up. But I'm going back to work on Monday."

Tom stood silently by, left out of the hubbub of Norah and Piper's reunion. He moved his suitcase from Norah's car to his then went to Sam's car to retrieve Piper's suitcase. He placed it on the steps to the house and walked back to Norah.

He kissed her lightly on the cheek. "I'll see you next week."

Norah barely acknowledged him leaving as she looked at the picture on Sophie's phone. "Aww, Pip, you look beautiful!"

Sam gave Piper a hug. "You have a good weekend with your mom, and we'll see you after school on Monday." He turned to Norah. "Thanks for this week. It was nice having so much uninterrupted time. And you look like you had fun. Nice tan."

Norah nodded, and when Sam and Sophie left, she moved the suitcases inside. Piper did not stray from her side as Norah unpacked.

"The cabin was so pretty for Uncle Joe and Aunt Emma's wedding. There was a gigantic Christmas tree with white lights and red roses everywhere. Aunt Emma's dress was all lace and beads, like that one you took on the cruise. The men all wore tux..." She thought for a minute. "Tux... I can't remember."

"Tuxedos?"

"Yes!" she shouted. "That's it. Daddy had a green tie, and Uncle Joe's was white. Did you like my dress?"

"I loved it."

"We bought it in Rhode Island. Des and Gracie helped pick it out."

"Did you have fun with them?"

"It was the best. They got me so many presents. I left them at Daddy's because I have toys here. Did you go swimming? Was the water warm?"

Norah chuckled to herself. Piper had always liked to spin from one topic to another. "The water was so warm I thought I was in a bathtub." She described the fish they'd seen and showed her pictures she'd taken.

"Will you take me on a cruise sometime?" Piper asked.

"Definitely." They sat on the couch to read a book.

At the end of the book, Piper crawled into Norah's lap. "Tom's nice. I like the horses he gave me."

"They were a nice present. You needed them for that stable."

"Do you love him?"

"Love him?" Norah's breath caught. "No, I don't think I'd say that."

"Daddy loves Sophie. They say it to each other all the time. And he kisses her while they're cooking."

"Ooh, mushy stuff." Norah chuckled.

"Yeah, but it's okay. I love Sophie too." Piper looked at Norah with eyes wide. "Is that okay?"

"Of course it is. Our hearts have enough love for lots of people."

"I don't love Tom." She still looked serious.

"You don't know Tom very well. You've known Sophie for almost a year. Love takes time." Norah stood. "Let's get you ready for bed. I'm looking forward to sleeping in my own bed."

Piper climbed into bed. "Will you sit with me until I fall asleep?"

Norah sat next to her, looped her arm over Piper's shoulders, and drew her close. "Of course. I missed this."

Piper was almost asleep when she whispered, "Will Tom move in here with us like Sophie moved in with Daddy and me?"

"I don't think this house is big enough for three people. Do you?"

"No, there's no extra room here like there is at Daddy's. Sophie doesn't sleep in that room anymore. She sleeps with Daddy. She's been doing that since Uncle Joe came up to build the ramp."

Norah stayed until Piper's breathing evened out then went to the kitchen. She opened the refrigerator and eyed the wine bottle. *No, that's the last thing I need.*

Opting to skip the wine, she sat in the living room, in the glow of the Christmas tree she would take down the next day. Joe had come up in October to build the ramp for Sam. Piper had never mentioned that Sophie had moved from her own room to Sam's.

Piper's getting better at keeping secrets than I realized. That's one I wish she hadn't kept. Then I would not have been so surprised

43

when Sam and I had lunch. Or by his engagement. It really is time to move on. But what do I do about Tom?

On Monday, Norah returned to a full inbox and a desk scattered with papers. She was still working her way through them at lunchtime, picking at the salad her assistant had brought for her, when there was a knock on the door. Before she could respond, the door opened, and Tom sauntered in.

He smiled as he sat down in the chair facing her desk. "Looks like you're even more slammed than I am. Everyone wants their project to be the first in the new year. Did you and Pip have an enjoyable weekend?"

I don't like him calling her Pip. He doesn't know her that well and hasn't earned that right.

She also didn't like him walking into her office without an invitation. When they were working on the snow-making project in the fall, Norah's assistant, Ava, had been sick, and Norah had found it easier to leave her door open. Most people paused in the doorway and asked if she had a minute. Tom was one of the few who didn't, and at the time, it had made sense to her—they were working under a tight timeline and had formed their own shorthand. When Ava returned, Norah had gone back to working with her door closed, but Tom had continued to enter without stopping at Ava's desk.

I should have put a stop to it then.

"Yes, we had a wonderful weekend. Piper never left my side. How about you?"

"It was okay. I missed you. Let's go to that pasta place you like for dinner tonight."

He knew she didn't have Piper on Monday or Tuesday, and his assumption that they would spend the night together heightened Norah's annoyance. She wanted a night to herself. But she also knew what she needed to do.

"Pasta sounds good, but I won't get out of here until six, so I can meet you there."

"I'll make a reservation for seven o'clock, then you can go home and change. Why don't I pick you up? Then we'll only have one car. That'll be easier for wherever we end up afterward." He winked at her before standing and moving to her side of the desk. "You look so formal." She was wearing a black pencil skirt and a fitted blazer. Her blouse was white silk, and she had put her hair up in a bun. "Your island wardrobe was so sexy." He reached out to touch her hair. "Not that you don't look beautiful like this." He bent to kiss her cheek.

Norah rolled her chair out of his reach and raised her hand. "We can't do that here."

Tom smiled indulgently. "Okay. I can wait. See you later."

She sighed as he closed the door. At midafternoon, she sat up straighter as she read through a proposal for an extra-high–voltage transmission through the state. Norah knew they had tried to put it through New Hampshire the year before.

She shook her head. *So now they're going to come across the river and pillage Vermont. Not if I have anything to say about it.*

Norah stepped on the brake and pushed the ignition button in her car for the third time. And for the third time, the car made no sound. She pawed through her tote bag until she found the fob. *Maybe the battery is low.* That had happened to her before. But even bringing the fob closer to the dashboard didn't help. She found the number for roadside assistance. It would be an hour before they arrived.

She returned to her office, punching in Tom's number as she walked. When his voicemail came on, she said, "My car won't start. Someone is coming to look at it, but I'm tired. Let's move dinner to another night."

Before she even got to her desk, her phone pinged.

"Hi," she said.

"Hi," Tom said. "Do you want me to come over? I can stay and then give you a ride to work in the morning."

"Oh, I'm not at home. I'm still at the office."

"I'll come there, then. Give you a ride home."

"That's not necessary. I don't even know what's wrong with the car. It might just need a jump."

"What if it's more than that? How will you get home?"

"I'll figure it out." Exasperation crept into her voice. "Look, if I need a ride, I'll call you. I have some work I want to start on while I wait. It's going to be an hour."

"Call me when you get home, please?"

"Tom, I'll be fine, but okay, I'll let you know when I'm home."

Two hours later, Norah was home, but her car was not. She'd called an Uber. The mechanic who checked out her car had said it should be ready the next day. A quick call to Ava took care of a ride to work in the morning. Then she lay on the loveseat, exhausted. She held her phone, thinking about Tom's request and his offer to give her a ride home. The last thing she wanted was a man who thought he had to come to her rescue or who wanted to always know her whereabouts. Reluctantly, she sent him a text, and when he responded, she ignored it.

What a start to the new year.

Chapter Five

The Breakup

Norah

THE HOST WALKED NORAH to the table where Tom was waiting. Before she left her office, she'd changed into jeans, a cream-colored V-neck sweater, and black boots with high heels. She rarely wore them in the winter, but they always made her feel invincible. Her hair was in a high ponytail because she liked the way it swung when she moved her head. Between the boots and the ponytail, she felt in command. And she needed that tonight.

"Your car's all fixed?" he asked.

"Yes. It needed a new starter. That was a good meeting this afternoon." Hi-Watts, the company proposing the high-voltage transmission line, wanted a preliminary hearing in April, and today marked the start of Norah's team prepping for it. "I'm glad you're on the team. You're the best lawyer on staff."

"I don't know about that, but I'm happy to be working closely with you again."

"Don't be modest," she said.

They discussed the project throughout dinner, and whenever the conversation veered into the personal, Norah steered it back to work.

Finally, as dessert was served—cheesecake for Tom and cannoli for Norah—he asked, "Should we go to your place or mine?"

"I can't see you anymore. Not in that way," Norah blurted. *I'm terrible at this.* She remembered how she'd told Sam she was moving out as he left for a work trip.

She watched the emotions crossing Tom's face. He brought his hand to his mouth. *Confused* was the look that finally settled in his eyes.

"What are you saying?" he asked.

"I don't want to date you." It was easier to say the words now that she'd broken the ice.

"I thought we were beyond dating. Dating is what you do when you're sixteen." His face went from confused to indignant.

49

"Whatever you want to call it, I don't want to do it anymore." Norah worked to keep her voice calm.

"We're a good match. Our backgrounds are similar, we got along well on the cruise, and your parents like me. To say nothing of the incredible sex. Why would we stop?"

Norah took a deep breath. "It's not my parents who are dating you. Their opinion means nothing to me."

"You told me they tolerated Sam because he's Pip's father, but you knew they would have preferred you with someone more your equal. That seemed like it bothered you."

His use of Piper's nickname was like nails on a chalkboard. She struggled to keep her tone civil. "I prefer that you call her Piper. And really, my relationship with Sam is none of your business." Norah took a deep breath, opened her purse, and found the fifty-dollar bill she'd tucked in earlier. She placed it on the table. "That should cover my share of the meal. I enjoy working with you, but I've realized I don't want to be in a relationship." She pushed back her chair and stood. "And now I need to go home."

Tom stood and grabbed her arm before she could step away. "This is because of that night, isn't it?"

"What night?"

"The night before New Year's Eve. When you didn't get off."

"Jesus." Norah looked around. "This is hardly the place for that conversation," she whispered.

"Well, where would you like to have it, then? I know you won't do it at work, and you're about to walk away from something that could be great."

Norah struggled unsuccessfully to free her arm from his grasp. "It's not because of that."

Tom took a step closer. "Every other time was amazing." He leaned in and kissed her neck. "And New Year's Eve was beyond words. Don't let that one night derail us."

Norah yanked her arm away. "No." Not caring how she sounded, she hissed, "Every other time was *not* amazing. I faked it." After picking up her coat, she walked to the exit, hoping he was not following her.

Dammit. I did not want it to come down to that.

A week later, Norah scheduled another meeting to discuss the Hi-Watts hearing. This would be her first time seeing Tom since the night she'd walked out of the restaurant. She hoped nothing would change at the office. They were both adults. Relationships—oh, how she hated that word—ended, and life went on. She'd spent more time dwelling on his absence from her work life than she cared to admit. Since their first dinner date in the fall, he'd been a regular visitor to her office, but prior to that, it hadn't been unusual to go for two weeks—or even a month—without their paths crossing during the workday. She convinced herself that not running into him was completely normal and not because he was trying to avoid her.

Norah was always the first person to a meeting, and today was no different. She sat at the head of the conference table, chatting easily with the representatives from various departments as they trickled in. Legal was the last to arrive, and she was surprised when Wyatt, one of the other staff lawyers, walked through the door.

"Where's Tom? We agreed that he should be the one representing us at the hearing."

"He said he was swamped and asked me to attend today and take notes. Tom predicted you'd be concerned and said to tell you not to worry." He smirked at Norah.

She and Tom had not hidden the fact that they were dating, and by Christmastime, the entire department had known they were going on a cruise together. Norah had told no one that she was no longer dating Tom and didn't know if he had. She'd been sure, a couple of times, that Ava was going to ask why he didn't come around anymore.

She couldn't read Wyatt's smirk. *Does he know Tom and I are no longer dating?*

"All right, let's get started." Norah began the meeting by asking for pros and cons.

Ava recorded the responses, which included improving grid reliability and economic benefits from both job creation and lower energy costs.

Wyatt spoke up. "This is going to be transmitting hydro-electric power from Canada. It's clean energy and could reduce greenhouse gas emissions, which will combat climate change."

"There will be a scar on the entire spine of the state! It's not worth the clean-energy trade-off."

Norah was glad someone else had given voice to her major concern. "We've got two big positives. Let's list the negatives."

"The impact! It will disrupt wildlife habitats and have a negative effect on wetlands."

"Energy conservation, smaller renewable energy projects, and upgrading the existing infrastructure will benefit Vermont more."

"Speaking of benefits, Vermont will get nothing. The energy is all going to Massachusetts and farther south."

Norah loved it when the room sparked with passion. She smiled. "Let's make sure we've heard from everyone and then dive deeper to see if the negatives outweigh the positives. Anyone else have ideas?"

"There are studies showing health risks from the electromagnetic fields."

"It's going to be tremendously expensive. Could that money go somewhere else for a better benefit?"

When the flow of ideas stopped, Norah spoke up. "I'd like to spend the rest of the afternoon examining the corridor Hi-Watts is suggesting. We need to know every tree, every rock, and every bend in the river that could be affected. The hearing in April is very early in the project, but if we can provide convincing arguments for or against, we can save a lot of time, so I want us to be as prepared as possible."

At the end of the afternoon, the group had identified several significant wetlands that would be affected. Norah assigned areas of study and concluded the meeting. "We'll meet again in two weeks." She turned to Wyatt. "You'll bring Tom up-to-date? Tell him I'd like him to be here next time."

At the next meeting, Wyatt was the first one to walk into the conference room. Norah cocked her head, but before she could say anything, he raised his hands. "Tom's sick. He called out yesterday and today."

She shrugged. "Okay."

"Norah, I'm interested in this project, and I'm not without credentials. I minored in environmental science. Don't let your relationship with Tom color who you want working with you."

"I'm not!"

Wyatt smirked. "Whatever you say."

At the conclusion of the meeting, Norah remained at the table, considering Wyatt's words. *Why do I want Tom on the project? Because he's the best lawyer on staff. But is he? Wyatt has made significant contributions already. I should have known about his minor. I always vet whomever I'm working with, and I didn't do that for him. Do I have lingering feelings for Tom that are interfering with my judgment? I should never have gone to dinner with him. That was my first mistake.* She pushed back from the table, shaking her head. Her life had gotten messy, and she didn't like it.

The next day, an email arrived, announcing the resignation of Tom Sindal. Norah sat up straighter and read it again. The email didn't specify where he was going but indicated he had cleared up all his pending work the week before and would use vacation time to cover his two-week notice. There would be a reception the next morning from nine to ten, to allow people to wish him well in his new endeavors.

Norah walked into the break room shortly before ten, and as she had hoped, there were only a few people still standing around chatting. She poured a cup of coffee and made her way to Tom, who had just said goodbye to the head of the legal team.

She put her cup on the table and extended her hand to Tom. "I'm sorry to see you leaving the agency."

"Are you?"

"Of course I am. I hoped we could continue to work together. Who's going to be the beneficiary of that superior legal mind?"

"You thought we could work together after what you said as you walked away?" His voice was dripping with venom. "I'm sorry. No. And as far as where I'm going, I'll be in a place where my talents will make a difference." He walked away, leaving

Norah standing by herself. "Hey, Jonathan," Tom said in a jovial tone. "I'm going to miss you. We need to get out on the golf course if summer ever comes." He clapped Jonathan on the shoulder.

Norah felt his eyes follow her as she left the break room.

Chapter Six
A Spa Day

Norah

NORAH REACHED FOR THE baby her friend Caitlin Ortega was cradling in her arms. "Look how big he's gotten. Let me hold him." She snuggled the baby close to her chest. "Hi, Matty. It's been way too long since I've seen you." She kissed the top of his head then looked back at Caitlin. "I can't believe I haven't seen you since before Christmas."

"I know." Caitlin wrapped her arms around Norah and the baby. "It's been too long. Matteo is six and a half months old, and he's missed his auntie Norah." She grinned. "Let's get some coffee. Jesse will be back soon, and then we can take off."

Norah sank into a chair and settled Matty on her lap. "Will he be happy here?"

Caitlin placed a mug on the table in front of Norah. "He loves being held, and with two older sisters and an older brother, plus Jesse and me, he's very indulged."

"I'm so glad you suggested having a girls' day. And taking a day off from work for it makes it feel even more decadent."

"Between Diego's travel baseball schedule and the girls' skiing, we've been tied up every weekend. I need a Norah day. And thankfully, Jesse recognized that."

"He's still earning those 'greatest husband ever' points." Norah chuckled as she took a sip of her coffee. "Piper loves skiing with Toni and Janey."

"We're having a lot of fun. Sam hates that he can't go with them because of his ankle." She looked warily at her friend. "How are you feeling about his engagement?"

"I'm okay. He made it clear in the spring that he wanted to be married, and since I will not take that step, we weren't going to last long-term. Do you like Sophie? I mean, I do. She's great with Pip, but I still feel protective toward Sam."

"They're good together. Sam's done a lot of work on himself over the last year, and I think she has too."

Norah nodded. "Do you know what their wedding plans are? This is hard to believe, but Pip has become a secret keeper. She tells me very little about her father."

"Janey's gotten good at secrets too." Caitlin chuckled. "The wedding will be in Rhode Island, at Sophie's parents' restaurant. In June, but I don't know the exact date. Probably after school finishes for the summer. You need to tell me what happened between you and Tom. I need the complete story."

Norah heard Jesse come in. "When we get to the spa."

Jesse greeted Norah with a kiss on the cheek as Matty laughed and waved his arms at the sight of his father. "Let me take him, and then you ladies can be on your way. It's good to see you, Norah."

Three hours later, after enjoying massages, Norah and Caitlin were relaxing in a saltwater pool with a view of the snow-capped mountains of the Presidential Range in New Hampshire.

"Ahh." Norah sighed. "This is nice, and I needed it as much as you did." She looked at Caitlin. "The last massage I had was on the beach of the cruise line's private island, with steel drums playing in the background."

"And Tom by your side?"

"Yes. It was an outstanding experience."

"And then…"

"And then… he told me he'd like to help me give Pip a sister."

"Say what?" Caitlin's eyes were wide.

"He always thought he'd like a second family, and I'm the extraordinary woman he'd like to do it with."

"Wow. What did you say to that?"

Norah told her about being caught in the riptide, and how Tom had helped her overcome the fear of getting back in the water. "I'd been gazing into the flames of a bonfire on the beach, thinking that maybe it could work out with him. I didn't think he'd try to dominate me." She sank under the water, then surfaced, pushed her hair away from her face, and looked at Caitlin. "And then he came out with that. I couldn't say anything—I was so surprised. You know how Sam always complained about how icy my tone could be?"

Caitlin nodded.

"I didn't want to do that. If I'd tried to get out the words, 'I never intend to have another child,' I would have sounded like a total bitch. So I said nothing. When have I ever been afraid to articulate what I want or don't want? I'm so angry with myself." She squeezed the water from her hair.

"I've never known you to hold back."

"We had two nights left, and you know how... I'd been faking with him?" Norah had shared all her frustrations about Tom with Caitlin.

Caitlin nodded again.

"I didn't fake that night."

"Well, that was one way to let him know how you felt."

Norah shrugged and shook her head. "Not really. I withdrew the next day, and he thought it was because of my lack of orgasm the night before. That was New Year's Eve. We had this phenomenal five-course meal with wine pairings, and I might have had a little too much wine. I ravaged him on our balcony."

"Ravaged?" Caitlin grinned.

"I was going to get what I wanted, come hell or high water. That was a mistake. It made him think everything was fine between us. I gave him the expectation that our relationship would continue and maybe even that we'd have a baby. And that was the last thing I intended."

Caitlin put her hand on Norah's arm. "How did he react when you ended it?"

"He left the agency. I hoped we could work together, but he had other plans. Let's go into the sauna." After they settled in the heat, swathed in towels, Norah said, "I'd already made up my mind to end it. I agreed to go to dinner, and when we finished, he asked, 'Your place or mine?' Not in so many words, but he was so presumptuous. And there it was—the first step to him dominating my life."

"It doesn't have to be that way. You could be partners." They'd had this discussion before.

"Not every man is Jesse Ortega."

"Just like they aren't all Bennett Taylor." Caitlin knew Norah despised the way her mother bowed to her father's wishes. "You and Sam were good partners."

"We were. For a while, anyway." Norah sighed.

"You never told him, did you?"

"No." Norah closed her eyes.

"Do you ever regret it? Because you're an excellent candidate for reversal. It's only been four years."

With her eyes still closed, Norah said, "My feelings haven't changed."

When Piper was three, Norah had needed to make a business trip to California. Her meetings lasted two and a half days, but she'd told Sam she needed to be there the entire week. She went directly from her last meeting to a hospital, where she had her tubes tied. She stayed two more days to make sure there weren't any complications then took the red-eye home on Friday night. Piper launched herself into Norah's arms as soon as she walked in the door. Norah was aghast because she wasn't supposed to lift more than twelve pounds and felt guilty about what she was going to keep from Sam. The first words out of her mouth attacked the condition of the house. That rift had lingered for weeks—long enough for her to heal completely from the surgery.

Norah opened her eyes. "I watch you with Matteo. You were born to be a mother, but I wasn't, for so many reasons. I loved holding Matty this morning, snuggling him, drinking in that baby scent, but it didn't stir any yearnings. I'm at peace with my decision. Sam was pushing for another baby, and eventually, he would have convinced me. I couldn't let that happen. I didn't tell him because I knew it would destroy our relationship." She scoffed. "Little did I know that my silence would derail us. I've worked all that out. I know I was a bitch to him and treated him like he couldn't do anything right, but truthfully, he did it all better than I did. That killed me. I'm a much better mother now than I was before. Pip is my whole heart, but I don't want more children."

"I've told you before how much it means that you shared this with me." They'd gone on a girls' weekend two years before, and Norah had told her the whole story.

"It's meant a lot, having someone to talk to. And I appreciate that you haven't told Jesse. I know you don't keep secrets."

"So, what now that you've finally had to accept that it's over with Sam?" Caitlin studied her. "You have accepted that, right?"

"Yesss." Norah stretched out the word like a rubber band. "I don't even think I'm going to date. Work is busy, and I'm going to be the best mom I can be. Since my first date with Tom, I've had conflicted feelings, but now I'm over it."

"You're going to miss the physical side of things."

Norah laughed. "I've got my vibrator." She continued laughing. "What about you and Jesse? Any chance you're going to get careless again?"

"That's a big no. Jesse had the snip right after Thanksgiving. We received the all-clear last week. He's got no little swimmers left."

Both women laughed.

Chapter Seven

Revenge

Norah

NORAH MANEUVERED HER CAR into the tight parking spot, muttering to herself. "Just another reason I'm glad I don't work in Montpelier anymore." She grimaced at Ava, who had ridden with her. Vermont would hold the preliminary hearing for the Hi-Watts project in one of its office buildings in the state capital.

"I don't know why we insist on calling this a hearing. It's more a chance for all the parties involved to lay their cards on the table." Norah had always thought there could be a better format for the preliminary exchange of information.

"But there will be lawyers. They will swear in the people giving testimony. But no judges. Right?" Ava had attended several of these hearings since she'd become Norah's assistant.

Norah sighed. "You've got it right. I like how much you've learned. I've been meaning to tell you that. Today's 'hearing' will have a panel of three commissioners overseeing it. I wish we could streamline the system, so we don't waste everyone's time. Unless Hi-Watts changes their plans, this entire process will take a couple of years."

"Think there's any chance they'll withdraw?"

"I'll be surprised if they do. But we've got good arguments to present, and so does the Agency of Natural Resources, so maybe."

They settled in the conference room, and Norah went over her notes. Her team was going to focus on the theory that conservation, smaller renewable energy projects, and the upgrading of aging and overloaded infrastructure would better serve state of Vermont. The Agency of Natural Resources would discuss the harm to wetlands, and Fish and Wildlife would cover the damage to wildlife habitats.

The Hi-Watts group drifted in, filling the seats on the other side of the room from the state agencies. The hearing was to convene at ten o'clock. At five minutes to ten, Norah heard Ava gasp. She turned to see what was going on and saw Tom taking his place at the table with the Hi-Watts representatives.

Ava whispered in Norah's ear, "Did you know he was working for them?"

Norah shook her head. "I had no idea."

Without missing a beat, Wyatt stood. "If it please the panel, I need a brief delay, no more than fifteen minutes." The delay was granted, and Wyatt motioned for Norah to follow him. He led her into a small office. "You're no longer dating him?"

"No." She was indignant.

"I had to ask. None of us were sure what was going on between you."

She raised her hands, exasperated.

"I know. Your personal life is none of our business, but you know how office gossip goes. We wondered. I can ask to have him removed," Wyatt said.

"Do you think that's the best course of action?"

"He was part of the preliminary discussions. Before he resigned, I briefed him on the meetings he didn't attend. That could provide Hi-Watts with an unfair advantage."

"Let's think about this." Norah ran her hand over her mouth. "None of the arguments we're making are unexpected. Hi-Watts had a good idea of what the problem areas were before we started. Even if we ask for Tom to be dismissed, he's already shared what he knows. Removing him will postpone today's hearing. That's already happened once, and here we are in May. This could drag on indefinitely. Let's go forward."

"I don't like it," Wyatt said.

"Are you uncomfortable going up against him?"

"No."

"Can we ask to have him removed at a later date?"

"Yes."

"Then let's go with that," Norah said.

Hi-Watts presented first, explaining the project and its benefits. Tom led them through their presentation, and Wyatt asked for clarification on points that were unclear. The Agency of Natural Resources went next, followed by the Fish and Wildlife Department.

Norah took the stand and talked about Vermont's climate initiatives. "The state is focusing on conservation and small renewable-energy projects. These fit the rural nature of Vermont. We also recognize the need for an upgrade of our transmission facilities. The Hi-Watts project will contribute nothing toward those goals. Yes, the hydroelectric power this line will carry is 'green' power, but Vermont will not reap any benefit from it."

Tom had not asked questions of the other agencies, but when Norah finished, he stood. "Ms. Taylor, how long have you been head of the Agency for Climate Initiatives?"

"Since its inception, last year."

"What was your position before that?"

"I was deputy head of the Agency of Natural Resources."

"Climate Initiatives is a smaller agency with a smaller budget. Why did you make the move? Wasn't it a downgrade?"

"It was a lateral move and a better fit for my interests." *My God, he is using the discussion from Christmas dinner. How far is he going to go?*

"Your salary is less there, even though you are the head. Is that correct?" Tom asked.

"Yes."

"That must have been a difficult choice for a career-minded person such as you."

Norah fought to control her anger. "Benefits are not always financial. The office is closer to my home, so my commute is shorter and less costly. That fits my desire to use limited natural resources wisely."

Tom smirked. "One final question. Is it true that if you had not moved to a different agency, you would have been fired by the Agency of Natural Resources because of your strident refusal to compromise with views in conflict with yours?"

Norah remembered their drive to the airport and how she had confessed the true story of her move. She'd thought she could trust Tom. *I've never made such a huge mistake in my choice of a man.* "Yes."

Ava was quivering with rage as she and Norah walked back to the parking lot. A black woman, Ava wore her hair in tight, springy coils, and they bounced as her head was in constant motion, first looking at Norah then shaking in disbelief. She kept up constant chatter as Norah walked in stunned silence.

"What an asshole. He ambushed you. We've all been wondering if you were still seeing him. We thought maybe that was why he left—so there wouldn't be any conflict. Obviously, we had that wrong." They reached Norah's car. "Do you want me to drive?"

"No. Driving will give me something to concentrate on other than how I'd like to strangle him."

"That's what I want to hear!" Ava said as Norah steered the car onto Route 89. They were almost back to White River Junction when Ava made a request. "Stop at the Sidecar. We need a drink."

Norah didn't argue, and fifteen minutes later, a server was placing two margaritas in front of them. "I ended things with him on our second day back to work after the cruise. It wasn't anyone's business—that's why I didn't say anything."

"It's no excuse, but you know how the office gossip is. I guess he wasn't happy with you breaking up with him?" Ava asked.

"No. I was stupidly naive enough to think we could work together. I found out I was wrong when I went to wish him well on his last day."

"What did you say to make him go after you like that?" Ava had finished her first drink, and the alcohol loosened her tongue.

Norah blushed. "You could say I undermined his manhood."

"Ooh mama," Ava hooted. "I need the deets."

Norah shook her head. "I've told you enough. Use your imagination."

Ava's face turned serious. "How did he know all of that? And is it all true?"

When Norah moved to the Climate Initiatives Agency, Ava was the first person she'd hired, but the young woman didn't know Norah's history.

"Sadly, yes, it's true." Nora told Ava about stopping for dinner at her parents' house and how her father had run his mouth. "When we were back on the road, Tom asked me about it, and obviously, I told him more than I should have. I thought I could trust him. I'll never make that mistake again."

"Was it as bad as what he said? Were you going to be fired?"

"I clashed with the head of the agency. He was new—had been there about six months—when things reached the boiling point. Part of it was that I'd hoped to be named head, but the bigger issue between us was that he wanted to compromise on every issue. I thought we should take stronger stands. Our relationship became extremely acrimonious, and he finally told me I could move to the new agency or leave. Tom twisted it to make it sound worse."

"His sole purpose today was to humiliate you, wasn't it?"

"It felt that way. I won't let my guard down again, that's for sure."

Chapter Eight

Tattoos and a Pup

Norah

NORAH SURVEYED THE LOT that her cottage sat on. Trees on the north and south borders gave her privacy, but the neighbors were close enough that she didn't feel isolated. A small knoll captured her attention, and she remembered watching Piper try out the skis Sam had given her for Christmas the first year they were separated. By the end of that winter, Pip had been regaling her with tales of riding on the chairlift.

The raking was done, and Norah was considering making flower beds in the front. It had been too late to plant a garden when she finalized her purchase of the property the year before, and she missed the color that flowers added.

The former owner had left his gardening tools, and Norah found a spade and used it to cut away the sod on both sides of the stairs leading to the front porch. She picked up a hoe and attacked the soil, making it ready for plants and releasing the anger still roiling from the hearing the day before. Winded, hot, and dirty, she sat on the steps, contemplating what to plant. She decided that, after a shower, she'd drive over to a nearby nursery that had opened two weeks earlier.

Should I wait until next weekend when I have Pip? She smiled, thinking back to how many trips to the nursery it used to take when she'd gardened at the other house. *I'll get things started, then Pip and I can go back next weekend to buy more.* Hair had escaped from her messy bun, and she brushed it away from her face. *I'm a mess. Two hours digging in the dirt will do that. A shower is going to feel so good.*

After leaving her filthy clothes in a pile, she walked through the house to the bathroom, where she caught sight of herself in the mirror. Her arms and legs were pink from being in the sun, and her face was smudged with dirt. It had been her first time in the sun since the cruise, and she closed her eyes as memories of the tropical air, warm turquoise water, and beachfront massage washed over her. Thoughts of Tom attacking her during the hearing quickly replaced them. *I misjudged him so completely.*

Shaking, she opened her eyes and took a deep breath. She ran her hands over her front, shivering from the sensation. Cait was right. She missed the physical side of things but felt like she'd dodged a bullet with Tom.

She stepped into the shower and stood just out of the water, waiting for it to get hot. The water heater was in the basement, directly below the bathroom, and it rarely took long. After sticking her hand into the stream, Norah yanked it back as the still-cold water hit it. She tested it every few seconds for another couple of minutes, played with the faucet, and finally accepted that something was wrong. Moving under the showerhead, she quickly soaped and rinsed her body then turned the water off.

Wrapped in a towel and shivering, she dried off, wondering what the problem could be. After exchanging the towel for her robe, she walked to the basement and checked to see if the breaker of the water heater had been tripped. Finding it okay, she dressed in clean shorts and a T-shirt then went outside to sit on the porch. She was still cold from the shower, and the sun would warm her while she figured out who to call.

This was the first problem she'd had in almost a year of owning the cottage, so she didn't have a list of tradespeople. Sam's father had forced him to assist with renovation projects as a teenager, and although Norah knew he hated it, he'd learned valuable skills that he used to remodel their house. *And he was able to fix anything.*

Norah sighed. She could have called him, but he and Sophie had taken Piper to Rhode Island for the weekend. And she would not do that even if he were home. Norah could take care of herself. Searching on her phone, she found several plumbers. She scanned the Yelp reviews for each and selected a few. Every call ended in voicemail—not unusual for a Saturday. Two of them called her back, telling her they couldn't get to her until Monday or Tuesday. Defeated, she contemplated cold showers for the next two days.

In a last-ditch attempt, she tried Ava and left a voicemail. "Hey, remember back in the winter when you had that broken pipe and somebody who knew somebody hooked you up with a guy to fix it? There's something wrong with my water heater, and I can't get a plumber out here until Monday or later. Do you think that guy might be available? I don't care what it costs."

Ava called back a few minutes later. "I called the guy. His name is Shane Hilliker. He'll come and look at it, but he lives a bit north of you, so it might take him some time to get there. I gave him your address. It's not his full-time gig, but he did a good job for me."

"I'm happy to find someone who'll come out today. The other plumbers I talked to didn't regard *no hot water* as an emergency."

Ava laughed. "You know you can come over here for a shower."

"That's very kind, but I'll be okay." The debacle with Tom had made Norah leery of blurring the lines between her work and personal lives, even if she and Ava had decompressed over drinks the night before.

An hour later, an orange Toyota Tundra with a kayak in the bed turned into Norah's drive. She watched from the porch as a tall, broad-shouldered man stepped out of the truck. His dark-brown hair reached below his shoulders, and he sported well-trimmed facial hair. He was wearing jeans with well-worn work boots and a black T-shirt. He loped across the yard to the porch.

"Shane Hilliker." He extended his hand. "You've got a problem with your water heater?"

She grasped his hand. "Norah Taylor. Yes, I tried to shower earlier and had no hot water."

"Probably an element. Let's take a look."

Norah hesitated. She hadn't considered that she was going to be taking a man she didn't know into her basement, with no one else around. *What's the difference between the basement and right here on the porch? Well, I could scream if he attacked me here. My neighbors might hear me.* She looked toward him. His right hand was resting on his jaw as he waited for her to make a move. Earlier, she hadn't noticed the tattoos covering his arm.

Shane raised his eyebrows. When Norah didn't respond, he said, "If you're uncomfortable being in the basement with me, just point me in the right direction. I assume that's where the water heater is."

The fact that he recognized her reluctance eased her apprehension. "Let me open the bulkhead. It's on the back side of the house. You can meet me out there." Norah walked inside, not wanting him to traipse through her house. As she unlatched the door and pushed it, she felt it rise effortlessly. Shane was standing at the opening and had pulled his hair into a bun while she was walking through the house. The water heater was in a far corner, and as they approached it, Norah was aware of Shane examining all the plumbing, which she knew dated back to the construction of the house more than sixty years ago. Her pre-purchase inspection had revealed some areas that needed repair but suggested there was no harm in deferring the work for a few years.

"I need to turn off the power before I test it." He strode to the breaker panel and flipped the one for the water heater. "Glad you've got them labeled. You wouldn't believe the messes I've seen." He knelt and pulled a multimeter out of his pocket. After a minute, he stood up. "Both elements are shot. You must have had problems before today."

"Not really." Norah shook her head. It felt like he was accusing her of something. She just wasn't sure what.

He glanced toward the walkout. "Mind if I look around before we leave?" Without waiting for her answer, he headed toward the washer and dryer. Reaching up, he jiggled the pipes. "How long have you lived here?"

"About a year and a half."

"Were these here when you moved in?" He waved his hand toward the appliances.

Norah nodded. Shane moved throughout the basement, stopping here and there to touch the pipes. Back at the bulkhead he said, "Let me close that. You latch it, and I'll meet you back on the porch."

She plodded through the house, nervous about what he was going to tell her and unsure of her comfort level with his abilities. When Norah joined him, he was sitting in one of the chairs.

"Do you live alone?" he asked.

Red flag. Norah didn't want to give him any more information.

He raised a hand. "I'm asking because if you live here alone, you might not have noticed the lack of hot water or how long it took to reheat, but if there are two or three people living here, showering, etcetera, you definitely would have been aware that you had a problem."

"My seven-year-old daughter is here two nights a week and every other weekend. I've always had hot water when I wanted it. Until this morning."

"Okay. Well, replacing the elements will fix the problem for now, but that heater is old. It won't be long until you have to get a new one." He reached up, pulled the elastic out of his bun, and snapped it onto his wrist as he shook his head to release his hair. "Your plumbing is a mess. It goes far beyond the water heater."

The water heater was an item the inspector had mentioned. "What are your credentials? Ava told me this isn't your full-time job." There was something about him that Norah didn't trust. *Who does he think he is, walking in here and criticizing my house?*

"My father is a master plumber. I worked for him long enough to qualify as a journeyman. I supported myself as a plumber for a few years." He looked at her. His eyes were deep brown, and Norah sensed he didn't like being challenged. "I know what I'm doing."

"What do you do now?"

"This and that. I've got the elements in my truck. Do you want me to do the work or not?"

"Yes."

"Okay, I'll get at it." Shane stood, and as he walked toward his truck, he turned his head back toward Norah. "Unlatch the bulkhead. I can go in and out through there."

He's bossy. I didn't even ask him how much it's going to cost or how long it will take. What the hell is wrong with me?

Norah unlatched the bulkhead again, and Shane was waiting. "I've got to drain the tank. If everything goes well, you should have hot water in a couple of hours."

A dog barked, and Norah's eyes narrowed in confusion. None of her neighbors had dogs, and the barking sounded close.

"That was Gibbs," Shane said. "Hope you don't mind. I hooked him on your back lawn. I can't leave him in the truck. Gibbs, come."

A caramel-colored dog, about a foot and a half tall, came into sight. His coat was curly, and he stood at the top of the stairs. He barked one quick woof in greeting before Shane petted his head.

"Go back and lie down, buddy." Gibbs wandered out of sight and Shane said, "I doubt he'll leave any mess, but if he does, I'll clean it up." He climbed down the stairs, carrying a toolbox and a hose. "I'll let you know when I'm finished."

Norah went back upstairs, feeling dismissed and thinking about how presumptuous Shane was to put his dog on her lawn without asking. Peering out one of the back windows, she could see the dog was on a long lead tethered to a stake in the ground. The back yard was large and sloped down to a gentle brook. There was plenty of room for the dog to roam. A metal water bowl sat within the dog's reach, and a large metal water bottle was lying on its side next to it. *I guess he's a responsible pet owner. That's kind of a froufrou dog for such a brawny guy. I would have expected him to have a pit bull or a Doberman.*

Uncomfortable having someone else in the house, she looked around for something to do. She finally settled on cleaning out a bookcase in the living room. As she sorted the books, filling a box to give to the library for their annual sale, she could hear Shane working. Metal clanged against metal, and an occasional curse word made its way upstairs. After more than two hours, Norah debated going to the basement. She guessed that it wasn't going well, based on the swearing, which had increased in volume and intensity. A movement outside the window caught her eye, and she looked up from her spot on the floor to see him striding across the lawn toward his truck. He'd taken off his T-shirt, which let her see not just his well-developed chest and abs but also a large tattoo on his back. It appeared to be an open book and a tornado. Ink covered his right arm completely. The resulting sleeve stopped before his shoulder. He grabbed something then turned back toward the house.

Half an hour later, he called up to her. "I'm finally finished. Mind if I come up there and wash my hands?"

"No, of course not." She heard the bulkhead clang shut then his tread on the steps. "The kitchen is that way."

He'd put his shirt on, and his hair was back in the bun. After washing his hands, he splashed water on his sweaty face then pulled his T-shirt up to dry it. "That was a challenge. I'll hang out for a bit to make sure the water is heating."

"Okay. Do you want something to drink? Wine? Iced Tea? I don't drink beer, so I don't have any."

"You don't stock beer for the seven-year-old?" He grinned at her. "Do I look like a beer drinker?"

Norah blushed. "I... I guess I was making assumptions. Sorry."

"Iced tea is fine, and could I get some water for Gibbs? I'm going to get him."

When he came back, with Gibbs trotting alongside, Norah had placed two glasses on the porch table and a large pitcher of water on the floor. Shane filled the water bowl then joined Norah at the table. Gibbs noisily slurped his water then bounded onto the porch, heading for Norah.

"Gibbs, lie down." Shane's voice was firm, and the dog settled at his feet. "That water heater won't last much longer."

Norah didn't want to think about her plumbing. "What kind of dog is he? And how old?"

"A Mini Aussiedoodle. He's five."

"He's well-behaved." Norah searched for something else to say. "I'm surprised you don't have a bigger dog."

"The same way I should drink beer?" He raised his eyebrows.

Norah shrugged.

"I've got some free time if you'd like me to work on your pipes."

Norah blushed. "I-I need to think about that. What do I owe you?"

"Nothing."

"I'm not a charity case. I can pay you," she said.

"You really need a new water heater. I'm not sure I did you any favors, replacing those elements. I don't feel right taking your money."

"You were here three hours! On a Saturday."

Shane's refusal to let Norah pay him made her uncomfortable. She wondered what he was angling for. They sat in awkward silence until Shane stood up.

"Let's see if you've got hot water." He turned the faucet on and held his fingers under the flow. After a minute, he nodded. "That's better. You should be fine." He walked outside, bent over to pick up the water dish, then turned back to Norah. "Let me give you my number. For the next time you have a problem. Because I guarantee you *are* going to have problems."

She was holding her phone, reading a message from her sister Betsy, and Shane reached for it. Norah pulled the phone to her chest, frowning at him. Shane huffed a breath and lowered his hand.

"You know what? Forget it. Come on, Gibbs." He strode toward the truck and opened the door. Gibbs jumped in.

"Wait!" Norah called. "I'm not convinced my plumbing is as bad as what you're saying, but what's your number?"

As he called it out, she punched it into her phone.

Chapter Nine

Leaks Always Happen on Saturday

Norah

THREE WEEKS LATER, SAM knocked on her door. A couple of months after Norah had moved out, when the tension between them was still high, he'd started coming to her house for pizza on Friday when she had Piper, and Norah had gone to his house on Sunday when Piper was there. For well over a year, they'd continued the practice, although not as diligently now as in the early days. Sometimes Sophie came with Sam, but this Friday, he was alone.

Piper greeted him, as she always did, by jumping into his arms. "Daddy! Where's Sophie?"

Sam hugged her until she squirmed to be put down. "She's having a girls' weekend with her friends from the gym." He looked at Norah. "A bachelorette weekend."

"Not much longer now," Norah said. Their wedding would be the last weekend in June. "Are you having a bachelor party?"

"A bunch of us went to a Red Sox game last weekend and hit up a couple of bars. Nothing too wild."

"Piper's excited. I hear lots of wedding talk while she's here."

"I hope that doesn't bother you."

Norah shook her head. "It's fine. I'm happy for you, really." She checked on the pizza dough. "That needs to rise a bit more. Can I ask a favor?" When Sam nodded, she described the problem with her water heater. "This guy, Shane, made it sound like my basement is on the verge of being flooded, as all my pipes could fail at the same time. I'm not sure I trust him. Could you take a look?"

"Sure, lead the way." Sam walked around much the same as Shane had, touching the pipes here and there. "Your furnace is new. That's good."

As they walked upstairs, Norah said, "The furnace is the one thing I wish wasn't new because I want to put in a cold-weather heat pump. That dough should be ready now. You can give me the verdict while I make the pizzas."

Sam leaned on the counter. "It's a mess, Norah. The pipes are old. There are several spots where repairs were done that aren't up to code. Your water heater is ancient. Tell me about the guy who replaced the elements. Is he a licensed plumber?"

"I don't know." Norah sighed and relayed what Shane had told her about his background. "Why wouldn't he be working as a plumber if he has the credentials? They make good money."

"How much did he charge you?"

"Nothing! And that's part of why I don't trust him. It felt like he thought I was too poor to pay him. He said he didn't do me a favor by fixing the tank. Who does that?"

"I would." Sam shrugged. "As a favor to a friend."

"He and I aren't friends. I met him that day."

Piper came into the kitchen. "I'm starving. Is the pizza ready?"

They focused on Piper for the next couple of hours. After tucking her into bed, they returned to the kitchen.

"I'm not in a rush to get home. I don't think we finished the conversation about your plumber," Sam said.

"He's not *my* plumber!" She opened the fridge. "Wine?" Sam nodded, and she poured two glasses then walked out to the porch. "He's probably a drug dealer."

Sam's eyebrows rose.

"You should have seen him," Nora said. "His hair was longer than mine, and he had an elastic around his wrist to put it up in a bun. His right arm was all tatted up—a sleeve, I guess—and he had a huge tattoo on his back."

Sam suppressed a smile.

"What?" she asked.

"Shades of Mitzi. How'd you see his back?"

"He took his shirt off while he was working, and I saw him when he went to his truck to get something. He didn't tell me, but I'm sure it didn't go smoothly. There was a lot of swearing. And yes, I know I sound like my mother." Norah shook her head as Sam continued to smile. "There are guys at the agency with long hair, but his was extreme. He was bossy. And presumptuous. He hooked his dog on my lawn while he worked."

"Let me guess. He had a pit bull."

"Actually, it was an adorable Aussiedoodle named Gibbs."

"Very suspicious. All the drug dealers I know have poodle hybrids for protection."

"Shut up." Norah fought the smile trying to emerge. "He's got me staying awake at night, waiting for the sound of a water leak. And your analysis will not help."

"You asked. If you're really concerned, find a licensed plumber and have them give you an estimate. I guarantee it's going to be in the thousands of dollars."

She grimaced and stood. "I'm going to have another glass of wine. Do you want one?" Sam shook his head, and Norah wondered how long he was going to stay. When she came back, she said, "Let's change the subject. What's the wedding going to be like?"

Sam narrowed his eyes. "You really want to hear about my wedding?"

"I do. Marriage isn't for me, but I enjoy the party. Surely, you remember that. I loved most of the weddings we attended."

"It's going to be small, around fifty people. Just family and some close friends from up here. Sophie's parents own four restaurants, and the ceremony and reception will be at Whispers. That's their flagship. Jesse is going to be my best man, and Sophie's mom will be her matron of honor." Sam rubbed his jaw. "Sophie and Lydia have been through a lot. She was a teen mom. Sophie's father died when she was five, and they had it really rough until Charlie came into their lives."

"I'm surprised you aren't having one of your brothers be best man. Haven't you and Joe gotten close again? Piper is always talking about Joe."

"We have, and it was a hard decision, but Jesse's been there for me since I was twenty-three." Sam grinned. "I found another job for Joe. He's done one of those online minister things, and he's going to marry us."

"Piper showed me a picture of her dress. I love the periwinkle."

"Me too. Sophie wore a dress that color on our first date. Before Christmas, Joe told me how much planning their simple wedding was taking, and I've learned what he was talking about.

Charlie and Lydia are doing the legwork, but they consult us on every decision. At this point, I'm looking forward to the honeymoon. I'm grateful we're able to work out Piper's time." They had agreed she would stay with Norah while Sam and Sophie honeymooned and then stay with Sam and Sophie in August while Norah traveled with Betsy. Sam spun his empty wineglass between his hands. "I'm glad that we can talk like this."

"So am I." Norah considered what she wanted to say to him. "You're a great father, and I'm sorry that I didn't acknowledge that when we were together. You were much more present in Piper's life than I was, and truthfully, I was jealous of that, but I didn't know how to fix it. I think I'm a better parent now."

"I appreciate that. Thank you. When you left, I wondered how you were going to parent without me, with the hours you were working."

"The change to the new agency and less commuting time helped. Cait said you're trying to make a baby. I hope that works out for you. Pip will *love* being a big sister. I'm glad Sophie is in her life."

"We are trying for a baby. It's not happening as easily as it did for you and me. Ironic, isn't it?" He put his glass on the table. "I should head home." They stood, and he hugged her briefly. "Nice talk. Again, I really appreciate it." Sam started his car and rolled down his window. "I know you don't like me telling you what to do, but don't ignore the plumbing. If you don't want to hire the drug-dealing part-time plumber, find someone else."

"Yeah, you need to have some work done." The man reached overhead and tugged on the copper pipe. "That's not up to code." He released it and walked around the basement. "Neither is that. Or this." He pointed as he walked. "When was the house built?"

"In the fifties."

"Let's go upstairs." He rubbed his jaw as he leaned on the counter. "There are issues down there, no doubt. You said you want to invest to make it right, and that's a good idea. The problem is I'm booked solid for the next six months. There's a lot of new construction going on, and frankly, that's significantly easier than this job."

This was the fifth time Norah had heard the same story. Taking Sam's words to heart, she'd researched what needed to be done and the changes she wanted to make in the pursuit of being more environmentally friendly. She'd spent the last two weeks with a variety of plumbing professionals walking through her house.

"Thanks for coming," she said, discouraged.

"I can give you some other names. Mike Johnson or Rick Stevens. They do good work and have large crews. Maybe one of them would have an opening."

Norah smiled sadly. "I tried both of them, and it was the same story. Mike gave me your name."

"Building is really booming. I'm sorry. If you have an emergency—you know, a pipe break or something—you can call me. I'll try to get someone here, although I'm not guaranteeing anything. I already have a large customer base. And don't even bother trying me on the weekend. My guys work long hours, and they need Saturday and Sunday to regroup."

"If I want to get this job done, are you saying I should schedule it now for next year?"

"That's going to be your best bet. I can work up some numbers for you," he said.

"Let me think about it, and if that's what I decide, I'll be in touch. Thanks again."

Who the hell knew it would be as hard to find a plumber as it is to find a doctor or a dentist?

A week later, Norah opened her eyes to bright sunshine. *Sam's getting married today, and I'm surprisingly okay with it.* Dressed in yoga pants and a sports bra, intending to make the nine o'clock class with her favorite yoga instructor, she made a cup of coffee and savored her first swallow of caffeine as she broke two eggs into a bowl. She reached for her omelet pan and stopped midway when she heard an unfamiliar sound. *What was that?* Standing perfectly still, she listened but didn't hear it again. *My imagination is working overtime.*

She put butter in the pan, turned the burner on, and started to beat the eggs then heard the noise again. *What the hell?* She put the fork down and held her breath. Just as she was about to pick up the fork, it happened again. *No, no, no. It sounds like water dripping.* She went to the basement, where there was a small puddle fed by a drip from the pipe overhead.

Norah closed her eyes and breathed deeply. She opened her eyes and searched the shelves until she saw a bucket. After placing it under the pipe, she ran upstairs, where the butter was burning. She slid the pan off the burner and rubbed her forehead. Shivering from being in the cool basement, she stepped onto the porch, hoping the sun would warm her.

What the fuck am I going to do now? Why on a Saturday? She retrieved her phone and her cup of coffee then sat at the table.

An hour later, she had called each of the plumbers who had told her they didn't have the time to take on her job. No one was available to come and fix her leaking pipe. She scrolled and found Shane's number.

Chapter Ten

Shane's Social Skills Need Work

Shane

SHANE SQUINTED AT THE light coming through the window and pulled the blankets over his head. He'd worked until three in the morning on his latest project then stumbled to bed. Shoving the covers away from his face, he checked his watch. *Nine o'clock. Six hours of sleep. That works.*

He climbed out of bed, still wearing his shorts and T-shirt from the day before. He dropped to the floor and did thirty pushups then rolled to his back to do thirty crunches. His full workout would come later or maybe not at all. After peeling his clothes off, he started the shower, with ideas whirling in his mind. When he started something new, it became his total focus, and he was trying to guard against that. Today, he was going on a long, leisurely paddle. Days like this were rare, and he was determined to enjoy them. The project could wait until after dark, when he knew he'd be up late again. That would be his pattern until he finished—stay up late, get six hours of sleep if he was lucky, force himself outside, then back to work. He'd learned the hard way that taking some downtime was essential when he was deep into a project.

Gibbs was waiting when Shane walked down the stairs. "Ready to go outside, bud?"

He opened the door, and the dog bounded out. Shane raised his face to the sun. It was already a warm day. His kayaking trip would include a dip in the lake.

"Gibbs, come. We need to have some breakfast, and then we'll get on the road."

He followed the dog inside and picked up his phone, which had spent the night on the kitchen counter. Leaving his phone downstairs so he didn't pick it up as soon as his eyes opened was another strategy in his battle for balance in his life. In the three years he'd been doing that, he hadn't missed one important message. There were a dozen text messages and three voicemails waiting for him. He took a deep breath, held it for a few seconds, then blew it out. Glancing at the texts, he debated answering any of them. Nothing was urgent, and if he responded, a back-and-forth would develop, wasting his entire morning. They could all wait until later.

The first voicemail was from his agent. "Sometimes you forget you're awesome. This is your reminder." Shane smiled. Marcia sent something like this every morning, and it never failed to brighten his day.

His mother's voice came through loud and clear on the second. "Are you going to make it to our Fourth of July party?"

His parents always threw an enormous party for Independence Day, and Shane had missed it the last two years because he'd been traveling. He'd call her back in the evening. It would be fun to attend the party this year, even though it meant a trip across the country. It had been too long since he'd seen his siblings and their children.

The third message was from a number he didn't recognize. "Hi, Shane, this is Norah Taylor. I don't know if you remember me or not. You replaced the elements in my water heater back in May. I woke up this morning to a small leak in a pipe in the basement. Is there any chance you're available to fix it?"

Norah Taylor. Oh, he remembered her. He'd spent weeks hoping she would call asking him to replace all that dilapidated piping. Because while he did that, he could also get to know her better. Her apprehension about him had been obvious, but even that didn't overshadow how appealing she was—pretty, despite having endured a cold shower, and slightly awkward, assuming he drank beer and would have a big dog.

Fuckity, fuck, fuck. I had time back then to do the work for her. Now I'm tied up and won't be free for another six weeks. He punched the button to call her back.

"Hello?"

He liked the hesitation in her voice. "Hey, Norah, this is Shane. I can come over and take a look. How bad a leak is it?" It didn't really matter, but he wanted to prolong the conversation.

"I put a bucket under it, and there's less than an inch of water. It's been a couple of hours, so it's not bad, I guess?"

"Okay. I'll be there in an hour." Looking at Gibbs, he said, "We get to go see that pretty lady again." He filled his bowl. "Don't take all day eating that. We need to get on the road." Munching on a banana, Shane retrieved the tools he would need and loaded Gibbs into the truck.

Norah wasn't on the porch the way she had been back in May, so, leaving Gibbs behind, he strode to her door. When she opened it, Shane hoped he was hiding the attraction he felt toward her.

"Those pipes didn't miraculously heal themselves, huh?"

Norah rolled her eyes and huffed out a breath. "No. I unlocked the bulkhead so you can go through there again." As he walked away, she added, "Did you bring Gibbs? I can bring out some water for him."

"He'll appreciate that." *Dammit, I was hoping to talk longer, but she's all business.*

He headed down to the basement and surveyed the leak. When he heard her steps coming from outside, he turned around, and his breath caught. Her yoga pants clung in all the right spots.

"I forgot—I turned the water off, so I can't give Gibbs any. Did you bring some like you did the other time?" Norah stood awkwardly at the opening. "I could get it out of your truck."

"This shouldn't take long. He'll be okay. Surprised you know how to turn the water off."

Norah's facial expression quickly went from awkward to annoyed. "The little lady can't do such manly tasks?" She walked away without waiting for his reply.

Brilliant, Hilliker, just brilliant. The repair went more smoothly than the element replacement had. He took his tools back to the truck, disappointed that Norah was not on the porch.

Unhooking Gibbs, he said, "We need to apologize, big guy. I insulted the pretty lady." He looked up to see Norah watching from the doorway. "I didn't mean to insult you. There are plenty of men who don't know where the shutoff valve is located."

"Are you all done?"

"Yes. You're all set. I turned the water back on and shut the bulkhead. You need to latch it."

"Come around to the front, and I'll give Gibbs the water I owe him."

Norah was sitting on the porch with two glasses of iced tea and a bowl of water. As Gibbs slurped the water, she motioned toward the chair.

Shane sat. "Are you going to accept my apology?"

"I confess I've had several plumbers in here, trying to find one to do the work, and one of them showed me the valve." She sighed. "I'm frustrated by the whole thing."

"I must have missed your call." He kept his eyes locked on hers.

"I didn't think you were currently working as a plumber."

"Telling you I had free time to work on your pipes wasn't enough of a hint?"

Norah's face flushed.

"Or is it you want someone with lots of big shiny trucks and ten guys working under him, only one of whom has the experience I do? You want a 'professional' who's going to train his apprentices on your dime?" Shane did air quotes when he spit out the word *professional*. When Norah didn't answer, he stood. "Come on, Gibbs, let's go. We've got a lake to get to."

"Wait!" Norah called as Shane opened the door of his truck. "What do I owe you?"

"Nothing. Save it for the professionals. You're going to need it."

"This is the second time. I can't let you make repairs for me without paying you."

"Don't worry. It won't happen again."

Shane's intention, when he'd climbed out of bed, was to head to a lake north of his house. But the only thing he wanted as he left Norah's house was to find a body of water and get his kayak onto it as quickly as possible. Paddling would ease his frustration. He turned onto a road to a lakefront resort and found not just the resort but a public beach.

The kayak and paddle were quickly unloaded, then he strapped a life jacket on Gibbs. "I know you don't like it, buddy, but it keeps you safe." Gibbs took his spot on the kayak and looked accusingly at Shane, who climbed in without a life jacket. "It's right here." Shane pointed at the seat, where the jacket was serving as padding on the backrest. "I'll be fine."

He pushed away from the shore and glided silently through the water. *I'd be devastated if anything happened to Gibbs.*

Shane pointed his kayak north, drawing his paddle forcefully through the water, trying to displace the frustration he felt from his encounter with Norah. The lake's shoreline was sprinkled with vintage cottages, and he slowed down, wanting to study them. They were well maintained, and Shane estimated they'd been built a hundred years ago. Very different from the massive new builds he saw on the lakes where he usually paddled. The new "camps" were attractive and well landscaped but lacked the character he was seeing here. His breathing slowed, and he relaxed, drinking in the lake's tranquility. Best of all, there were no high-powered speedboats. A small wooden boat with an outboard motor, passing by on its way to the middle of the lake, had scarcely caused a ripple. Shane enjoyed the *putt, putt* sound the boat made, and he watched as the two men on board dropped the anchor. They cast their fishing lines out then settled in to wait for a bite from a hungry fish. Speedboats and their resulting wake were his primary motivation for putting a life jacket on Gibbs. He had never capsized but was well aware it could happen.

I feel like I'm back in the last century. This is nice. I'll come here again.

At the far end of the lake was an overnight camp for preteens. There was a lodge, and cabins were scattered over a large area. Shane watched as the campers had a rousing tug-of-war battle on the beach. He continued along the opposite side of the lake, where there were fewer cottages. As he neared the beach where he'd started, he admired a woman on a stand-up paddleboard.

"Think I could do that, Gibbs?" He wasn't sure his balance would be good enough. "I'll stay away from it because I'd have to leave you behind." He beached the kayak, pulled off his T-shirt, and strode into the water, with Gibbs by his side. When they'd both cooled off, Shane staked out a spot on the corner of the beach. "We'll dry off here before we head home."

His thoughts returned to Norah. *Why am I so bugged that she didn't ask me to do the work? It's not like I need the money.*

It's because she's pretty and I'm attracted to her. Working there would have given me an opportunity to get to know her, and it would have been an excellent distraction between projects. But I'm not sure her prettiness outweighs the prickliness. Her reaction to my crack about the shutoff valve was over the top. Shane knew he could be awkward, but usually, a heartfelt apology smoothed things over. *I won't hear from her again. I was a bit of a bastard when I left. My social skills need some work. That's what happens when you spend as much time alone as I do.*

Chapter Eleven

No More Tequila

Norah

"A TOAST!" WYATT RAISED his beer bottle. "To the good guys winning and the environment being preserved."

The people sharing his table clinked their bottles and glasses together, and someone said, "Hear, hear!"

Norah had gotten the notification earlier in the day that Hi-Watts had withdrawn their proposal, citing unfavorable geological findings. The team was jubilant as the word spread, and an outing to the Sidecar quickly came together. It was Friday night. They'd worked long hours, forging their arguments, and endured two hearings, including the disastrous one in which

Tom had blindsided Norah. They were all ready to blow off some steam.

Plates of wings, nachos, jalapeño poppers, sliders, bottles of craft beers, and margarita glasses covered the table.

"Unfavorable geological findings, my ass." Wyatt, the most vocal opponent to the project, had been like a ferocious bulldog, going after Tom during the second hearing. "They knew they couldn't win and would be tied up for years trying to obtain the necessary permits."

Norah sat quietly, watching the team celebrate their success. Most of them were younger than she was, in their twenties, and for some, this was their first significant victory. She remembered that feeling.

She leaned over to talk to James Collins, the president of an agency in the southern part of the state that had joined the fight against Hi-Watts. When Norah had called to tell him the good news, she mentioned they were gathering at the Sidecar to celebrate, and he'd made the drive north to join them.

"This one feels good," she said.

James nodded. "It does. Until the next company with no regard for the environment comes along. You did good work. If you ever want a change, let me know. I'd find a spot for you."

"You're right, of course, but I'm going to enjoy tonight." She celebrated with a margarita while she enjoyed the food then ordered a second one, which was half gone when people started to leave.

"We're going to head out. Are you ready to go?" Ava finished the last of her drink and leaned against Wyatt.

The three of them were the only ones left at the table. Norah appreciated Ava's concern about leaving her alone, but she also knew Ava and Wyatt wanted to get home for a private celebration. She'd enjoyed watching their romance develop over the past several months.

"I'm going to stay for a while longer. My parents aren't bringing Piper back until Sunday, so I don't have to hurry home," she said. A middle-aged man with a guitar had just climbed onto the stage. "I know Zeke, and I want to listen to him." She could see the hesitation in Ava's eyes. "I'll be fine. The crowd here never gets out of hand. I'm only going to stay for one set. Go. Enjoy the rest of the evening." Norah winked at Ava.

"Okay. I'll see you Monday."

"I can't wait to see what new dragons there are for us to slay." Wyatt swung his arm over Ava's shoulders, and they walked to the exit.

Norah finished her drink and asked for another one when the server picked up her glass. This was the most relaxed she'd felt since the year began. Hi-Watts was behind her, along with Tom Sindal. *I hope I never see him again.*

She and Piper had gone to Connecticut for the Fourth of July, and Piper had stayed for the week. It was the first time she'd seen her parents since Christmas, and it hadn't taken long for her mother to bring up Tom.

"I'm surprised you didn't bring Tom with you. I told some of my friends who you were dating, and they immediately knew who I was talking about. His family was very prominent and well respected before they moved."

Norah was relieved that at least her mother waited until Piper was off playing with her cousins before launching into this conversation. "I'm no longer seeing him."

"But you seemed so compatible. I don't understand."

"We discovered we want different things out of life, so we weren't as compatible as you thought."

"You're not getting any younger. You wasted eight years with Sam. Well, not totally wasted because we have our darling Piper, but you know what I mean. And you insist on living in that rural area. You will find no one there who's equal to you in stature—who's worthy of you."

"Mother, this conversation has gone far enough. There are plenty of wonderful people in Vermont, but it turned out Tom is not one of them. And I am perfectly content on my own. I can do what I want to and not have to defer to a man."

Norah returned to the present. *Thank God that's out of the way and Hi-Watts is in the rearview mirror.* The biggest remaining worry was the house. It had been two weeks since the last problem. *Tomorrow, I'll go through my list of plumbers and select one to call on Monday to get on their schedule for the winter.*

She would not include Shane Hilliker on that list. Norah had ruminated for days on his crack about her wanting to hire a professional. There was something appealing about him, but his snarkiness overrode it.

Zeke took a break, and Norah downed the last of her drink. It was time to go home, but she needed to visit the restroom first. Otherwise, she'd never survive the twenty-mile drive to her house without peeing her pants. When she stood, the third drink hit her, and she wobbled for a second, placing her hand on the back of the chair to steady herself. *Whoa.*

She came out of the restroom, still unsteady. *I think I need to have a glass of water and listen to a bit more of the music before I drive home.* She slid into her seat then looked toward the bar, hoping to catch the eye of a server. Instead, she saw a familiar head of long brown hair flowing over a broad back. *No, not here, please.*

"Could I get a glass of water with ice and a slice of lime, please?" she asked a passing server.

As Norah spoke, the man at the bar turned around, saw her, smiled, and raised his hand in greeting. Reluctantly, Norah acknowledged him, which was all the encouragement Shane needed to abandon his barstool, walk over to her, and sit in one of the empty chairs at her table.

"I didn't expect to see you frequenting a place like this," he said.

"What kind of places do you think I frequent?" *Why does he fluster me so?* She shook her head. "Actually, how do you in any way think you know me well enough to make a judgment on where I go?"

Shane raised a hand in surrender. "You're right. I don't know you well enough, but you seem like a swanky lady, and this can be a bit of a dive." He put his hand on the table. "Let's start over. Hi, Norah. It's nice to see you and not what I expected when I decided to stop in for a beer."

She rolled her eyes. "Hi, Shane. They serve the best nachos in the Upper Valley, and I like nachos." He wore khaki slacks and a white button-up shirt that accentuated his broad chest. The collar was open, and he'd rolled the sleeves up. A silver Rolex sat on his left wrist. "Nice watch. I don't remember you wearing that when you came to my house. Is it real?"

Shane snorted. "Of course it is. I don't fake anything. Do you?" His eyes sparkled.

He's flirting with me. I need to leave. Norah emptied her glass and stood up. "I'm going to head out." She swayed when she reached for her purse and sank back into her chair.

"How many of those have you had?"

Norah huffed. "Well, *that* is *water*!" She dug into her purse to retrieve her keys. "And I've had one. If it's any of your business."

Shane lifted the keys off her fingers. "But how many of those?" He pointed at the margarita glass still sitting on the table.

"Also none of your business. Please give me my keys."

106

"No." His voice was soft but deadly serious. "Your eyes are glassy, and you're unsure on your feet. You can't drive home."

"I am *fine*." As she spit out the words, she tugged on her keys, but his grip was firm. "Give me my keys."

"No. But I'll give you a ride home."

"Because you haven't been sitting in a bar, drinking beer, all evening?" *He is insufferable. Why does he think he's okay to drive and I'm not?*

"I've had that much." Shane pointed at his half-full glass. "My buddy is the bartender here. That's why I stopped, and I'd just arrived when you stumbled out of the restroom."

"I didn't *stumble* out of the ladies' room."

"If that wasn't a stumble, I'd hate to see what one looks like."

"I'm not drunk."

"You may not be." Shane shrugged. "But you're impaired, your house is a long drive away, and it's raining. You shouldn't be driving." He took a deep breath. "I'm not going to back down. The alternative is to sit here with me until you've sobered up." He held her gaze.

Before she could answer, the musician said it was time for another break and set down his guitar. He made his way to her table, pulled out a chair, and sat down. "Hey, Norah. I haven't seen you at a set in a long time." He fist-bumped Shane. "Good to see you." He wiggled his finger between Shane and Norah. "You two a thing?"

"No." Norah's reply left no room for discussion. "You know him?" Her glance went back to Shane.

"We're in a volunteer fire department together. I thought maybe someone had finally sunk their teeth into Shane. It would be a first."

Shane didn't say a word, but he continued to watch Norah.

"He did some plumbing work for me," she said. "And now he thinks he's my guardian angel. I'm trying to get him to return my car keys."

"Hate to tell you, sweetheart, but your eyes are glassy, and I can smell the alcohol. He's doing you a favor by holding onto your keys."

She'd met Zeke way back when she was getting to know Sam, Jesse, and Caitlin. *I guess that gives him the right to call me sweetheart.*

The server had brought over another glass of water, and she drank half of it while she weighed her options. *Which will be worse—sitting here until I'm sober or enduring the twenty-mile drive?* Because she knew Shane and Zeke were right.

Zeke was talking quietly with Shane while Norah tried to figure out what to do. He stood, ready to play his last set, then looked back at Norah. "Shane's a good guy. He'll get you home safely."

"Is Zeke's endorsement of my character enough for you?"

Norah huffed out a breath. "I suppose." She stood, putting all her concentration into being steady on her feet, and tilted against him despite her efforts. *I'm never touching a margarita again.*

"I've got you." Shane steadied her as they walked out the door and held her hand when she stepped into his truck.

"Is this electric?" she asked. The truck was silent as he turned out of the parking lot.

"It's a hybrid."

The effect of the alcohol was waning when they reached her house. Shane was out of the truck before Norah opened her door.

"I'm fine now. Thank you for the ride," Norah said.

He ignored her, walking with her to the porch and standing at her side while she unlocked the door. Norah thought of the first time Tom had walked her to the door. She wondered what it would be like to kiss Shane. She opened the door, and Shane pulled her car keys out of his pocket.

"Thank you for not fighting me." He handed her the keys. "I lost someone important to me when she drove after a night at a bar, and I made a promise to myself that I'd never let that happen again."

"I'm sorry." Norah cocked her head. "Do you hear that? Is it water running?"

"My God." He shoved past Norah. "It is."

Norah followed him to the basement door then down the stairs, where several inches of water covered the floor. She could see it pouring out of the water heater. Shane splashed his way to the shutoff valve for the house and then back.

"Dammit." He struggled with the valve. "I need a wrench." He dashed up the stairs and out to his truck. Norah was still standing on the stairs when he returned with a wrench and turned off the valve to the heater. "It's going to drain until the tank is empty. I'm sorry—there's nothing I can do tonight."

Norah rubbed her forehead as tears filled her eyes. *I will not cry. That is not what I do.* "Thank you. Let me get you a towel." They climbed the stairs. "I'm really grateful." The tears threatened again, and she turned away, trying to hide her vulnerability.

Shane used the towel to dry his feet and the bottom of his pants. "You'll be okay tonight. You'll have cold water but not hot. I'll come back in the morning, and we can discuss what you want to do."

"Do you want to stay here? You can sleep in my daughter's room."

What. The. Hell. Norah? Do you think you can trust him? But he'd come to her rescue, and it seemed pointless for him to drive home if he was going to come back the next day. The debate raged in Norah's mind. *I've had too much to drink. God, I hope he's smart enough to say no.*

"Gibbs has been home alone since early this morning. I can't leave him overnight."

Chapter Twelve

Norah Finally Hires a Plumber

Shane

"'THE BEST WAY TO find yourself is to lose yourself in the service of others.' That's from Mahatma Gandhi. Good meeting yesterday." Marcia's voicemail was surprisingly prescient because Shane intended to spend the day in service to Norah.

She tried to hide it, but she was on the verge of tears last night, and I don't picture her as someone who cries easily.

He'd been surprised when she staggered out of the restroom the night before. She was wearing a short white skirt with a purple tank top and didn't notice him enjoying the sight of her. He assumed she'd come straight from work and was with a bunch of colleagues. The Sidecar had a reputation for being a post-work gathering place. When he saw her sitting alone, he couldn't resist the temptation to join her. He certainly hadn't intended to insult her when he told her he was surprised to see her. But then she'd given it right back to him by questioning his watch. He laughed, remembering how Marcia had presented the watch to him during their meeting. There was no need for Norah to know he'd only had it for a few hours.

When she'd staggered again—*staggered* was probably too strong a word, but she was definitely unsteady—and taken her keys out of her purse, Shane had flashed back instantly to the last time he saw Alisha. The picture of her, keys in hand, sashaying out of the bar where they'd been partying, was as fresh as the day it had happened, even though fifteen years had passed. The next morning, he'd found out Alisha had died instantly when she wrapped her car around a tree. Norah wasn't the first person Shane had forcibly taken keys away from, and she wouldn't be the last. Shane would not lose another person because he was too much of a wimp to stop them from making a poor decision. Norah agreed without much of a fight, but he knew she wasn't happy. She didn't say a word the entire way to her house. The invitation to sleep in her daughter's room had been unexpected, and Shane had known it was the alcohol talking. As much as he would love to spend a night with her, it would not be like that.

Shane hurried through his morning routine so he could get on the road. He'd take Norah back to the Whistle Stop to retrieve her car then figure out what he could do to help her. They could pick up a water heater at one of the big-box stores. He should have told her to do that on his first trip to her house. The sight of Norah's car sitting in front of the house when he turned into her drive surprised him. It was early, not even nine yet, and he'd thought she would sleep in. Obviously, one more thing he'd had wrong about her. She probably never slept in.

He knocked on her door and stood patiently waiting with Gibbs at his side. She opened the door, and he tried to resist, but Shane's eyes traveled up and down her body. She wore denim shorts and a faded T-shirt from Columbia University. Her hair was in a messy bun, and her face was flushed.

"Hey, you already picked up your car. I planned to give you a ride back to the Whistle Stop."

"I couldn't sleep. At seven, I finally got up and called a rideshare to take me. Then I stopped and bought a wet vacuum, and I've been in the basement, trying to get rid of the water."

"How's it going?"

"There's a lot of water down there." She rolled her eyes.

"Can I take a look?" On the ride over, Shane had decided that he needed to shelve his take-charge attitude and let Norah lead. Asking for permission to return to the basement was the first step, and he followed her down the stairs. He could see that there were items that needed to be moved. "I can run the vacuum while you put things where you want them if that works for you."

After a couple of hours, the water was gone, and they were both hot and sweaty. Norah led him upstairs, poured two glasses of ice water, and walked out to the porch. Shane waited for her to say something, but she was quiet.

"If you want to hire me, I can redo all of your plumbing," he finally said. "I have something else I'm working on, so I won't be here eight hours a day, the way a professional plumber might be, but I'll get it done, and it will be done right. Your immediate need is a water heater, and we can probably pick one up across the river in West Leb. I can install that today. And I'll charge you if that makes you more comfortable."

And I'll be donating whatever you pay me to a charity. Probably Habitat for Humanity.

"I want to put in an on-demand water heater. Do you know how to install those?"

He nodded. "Do you want electric or gas?" He took his phone out of his pocket and started scrolling.

"None of my appliances are gas, so I want electric."

"May I come closer?" When Norah nodded, he moved his chair next to her and held out his phone. "These are in stock. I can drive over and pick one up."

"Can I go with you?"

"Sure. Let me shift a few things around." He took the blanket Gibbs usually lay on and moved it to the back seat. Gibbs watched him then jumped in when his spot was ready. Shane leaned in to whisper in his ear. "The pretty lady wants to go shopping with us. I couldn't say no to that, and I can't leave you here alone. So the back seat it is, buddy."

As they drove, Norah was more talkative than she'd been the night before. "Were you coming from work last night when you stopped at the Sidecar?"

"Not exactly. I'd been to Boston for a business meeting."

"What did you say you do?"

"I didn't." Shane guarded his identity carefully. "I dabble in a few different areas."

"Including plumbing."

"Now and then."

"I'm sorry you ruined your shoes wading through my basement."

"No big deal." He shrugged. "I wear them as little as possible."

By late afternoon, Shane had finished installing the water heater. He walked around the basement, trying to calculate how much time it would take to change out all the plumbing. His project was three-quarters finished, but he was very aware of his deadline three weeks away.

I can spend a few days here, hit the worst spots, then, after my deadline, work here full-time until it's finished.

He trudged upstairs. Norah had made chicken salad for dinner and invited him to join her. The tension between them seemed to be fading. "You've got hot water."

Norah smiled and extended her hand for a high five. "Thank you. I'm sure this isn't how you planned on spending your day."

Shane shrugged. "Let's discuss the rest of the work. As I told you this morning, I can do it. I'm in the middle of something, but that will be finished in a few weeks. I can work here a couple of days a week until I complete the other thing, and then I can be here full-time. Your furnace looks new, so that's a plus."

Norah's expression changed. "I want to put in a cold-weather heat pump. I want to reduce my use of fossil fuels." She redid her bun. "That probably sounds stupid to you."

"No, not at all. That's why I drive a hybrid." He thought for a minute. "Would you be okay with donating the furnace to Habitat for Humanity? I do some work for them."

"I like that idea."

"I don't have a lot of experience with heat pumps, but I can get my dad to come up and help me with it."

"Where does he live?"

"California."

"California! You can't ask him to travel all the way from the West Coast to work at my house!"

"It's not a problem. He and my mom love spending time here." He could see the hesitation in her eyes. "Seriously, he'll be happy to make the trip. Have you thought about how you'll supplement the heat pump? Because it won't keep you warm during the heart of the winter."

"I'm thinking about a pellet stove." She stood. "Come see." Norah motioned for him to follow her into the living room. "I think it could go right there." She pointed at the north wall. "I've been researching them. The house is small, so I won't need a huge one. It'll fit nicely."

"You've thought of everything. When do you want me to start? Do you want me to work when you're home or away?"

"I appreciate all that you've done for me." She looked chagrined. "But I don't know you very well, and I'm not comfortable giving you a key, so I prefer you work on the weekends when I'm here." Her face reddened. "I know that's asking a lot."

Shane shook his head. "I don't work a traditional schedule, so I'm fine with the weekend." He moved toward the door. "I'm going to head out. I'll see you next Saturday."

Chapter Thirteen

Braids and Boundaries

Norah

WHAT TIME IS HE going to arrive? We never discussed that.

By the time Piper woke up on Saturday, Norah had been up for over an hour after tossing and turning all night. This level of discomfort was unusual, and as Piper ate her breakfast, Norah tried to figure out what it was about Shane that bothered her. Maybe it was his supreme confidence. The way he had lifted the keys out of her fingers still rattled her, as did the way she'd succumbed to his command that he give her a ride home.

I never let anyone bully me like that.

"Mommy, a truck just drove in. Is that the man you told me about?"

Norah had told Piper there would be someone working in the basement but hadn't said anything about him. She was concerned about how Piper was going to react to his hair and tattoos. Sam's brother Matt had tats—Piper had told her that—but Norah didn't know if they were as extensive as Shane's.

This should be interesting. "Yes, that's him. Let's go outside and meet him."

"I like his orange truck. Why can't we have an orange car?"

Shane walked toward them, and Piper shrank behind Norah. He extended his hand. "Hi. I'm Shane. What's your name?"

"Piper," she whispered. Slowly, she extended her hand to shake his.

Shane turned his attention to Norah. "I thought maybe you were kidding about the seven-year-old." He grinned as Norah blushed. "Does she like dogs?"

"I love dogs." Piper didn't give her mother a chance to answer.

Shane walked back to the truck, and seconds later, Gibbs came bounding toward Norah and Piper.

"Gibbs. Stop," Shane said.

The dog immediately stopped, but his body was twitching in anticipation.

Piper looked up at Norah, who nodded, letting her know it was okay to approach the ball of fur. She dropped Norah's hand and ran to Gibbs, who continued to twitch but obeyed Shane's second command to stay.

"Piper, this is Gibbs. He'll lick you to death if you let him. You can pet him."

She reached her hand to the top of Gibbs's head, and Shane gave a tiny nod to let the dog know it was okay for him to greet the little girl. He sniffed her, and Piper dropped to the ground. She pulled the dog into her lap, and giggled as his tongue licked her.

"You've made a friend for life," Norah said. "She loves animals."

"I guess I've missed seeing her pets when I've been here. Or do they travel with her to her dad's?"

"We don't have any pets."

"Seriously? Every kid should have a pet. And especially a kid who loves animals." Shane stared at her. "Not even a hamster?"

Norah huffed. "A hamster? No. Animals are dirty and a lot of work." *Who does he think he is? How many weekends is he going to be here, and how much criticism of my parenting am I going to be subjected to?*

Shane shook his head. It was a subtle movement, but Norah saw it and suspected he didn't like her answer. "Piper, I'm going to hitch him on the back lawn while I'm working. He'll be on

120

a long lead so you can play with him. He'll like that because it will be boring for him while I'm working inside all day."

After Shane drove the spike into the ground and attached Gibbs's leash to it, Piper asked, "Why does he have to be hitched?"

"This is a strange place for him. If something scares him, he might run away. He's my best friend, and it's my job to keep him safe." Shane ruffled the dog's head. "Kind of like your parents keep you safe. Let's get him some water."

Piper was in and out of the house all morning, playing with Gibbs and trying unsuccessfully to have Norah join her. At noon, Shane retrieved the lunch he'd packed and sat down on the lawn to eat. Piper took her sandwich outside and sat down next to him. Gibbs was busy with a bone, and Shane explained to Piper that she should leave the dog alone when he was eating. Norah sat at the table, with a window open to keep track of what was going on.

"Your hair is as long as mine," Piper said.

"Yep, it is."

"Do you braid it or wear it in pigtails?"

Shane had pulled his hair into a bun when he started working. "Mostly a ponytail or like I have it now. Do you braid yours?"

"My daddy or my mommy does it for me."

"I see." Shane smiled. "I live by myself, so I don't have anyone to do it for me."

Piper studied him. "I could ask Mommy. She could do it for you."

Norah choked on her water.

Shane chuckled. "I think I'm okay."

Piper leaned closer to him. "Can I tell you a secret?" When he nodded, she confided, "Daddy is better at braids. He does buns too. He learned when I started dance lessons."

"A better bun than this?" Shane motioned toward his hair.

Piper studied him again. "Yes. You can't have any loose hair. The teachers get mad if you do."

"Well, then, it is a good thing I'm not taking dance lessons."

In the late afternoon, Norah heard Shane close and latch the bulkhead then climb the stairs to the kitchen. He washed his hands, and as he dried them on a towel hanging close by, he said, "The northeast corner is finished. I'm going to head home."

"How long do you expect it to take?"

"If all goes well, there's probably ten days of work." He sighed. "But it's not unusual for things to not go well, so it could be longer." He pulled the elastic out of his hair. "I hate being held to a schedule."

"Are you coming back tomorrow?"

"Yes." Shane walked to the back of the house to unhook Gibbs, and Norah followed. "And my dad will be here in October to help me with the heat pump."

"Oh."

Piper jumped up. "Can I walk him to your truck?"

"We can take him off the leash. He'll walk along with us." Gibbs walked between Shane and Piper, leaving Norah behind.

"Shane, wait." When he turned around, Norah said, "October is awfully far away. I mean... I thought..."

"My parents like to come when the foliage is at peak color." His answer left no room for discussion.

Norah fumed as she cooked dinner. *October? Surely I can find someone to do it sooner. He's so arrogant. He didn't even ask if that would be okay. If I find someone else to do the heat pump, will that piss him off so he won't do the rest of the work?*

Piper broke into her thoughts. "This was the best day. I can't wait until tomorrow so I can play with Gibbs again."

The next day went much the same except that Shane had two kayaks in his truck bed.

Piper ran to meet him. "What are those?"

"They're kayaks. Have you ever been kayaking? There's a lake near here. I'm going to go this afternoon."

"Daddy and Sophie take me paddleboarding there."

"It's the same idea except you're sitting in the kayak. Who's Sophie?"

"My daddy's wife. They're on a honeymoon."

Shortly after eating lunch, Norah heard Shane on the stairs and went to the kitchen, where he was washing his hands. She cocked her head. "Are you done?"

"Yup. I reached a good stopping point. It's a hot day, and I want to get out on the water. Why don't you and Piper come with me?"

"Kayaking?"

"Yeah. I have two, and they both have room for her."

"No, we can't do that."

"Can't we, please?" Piper asked.

"No."

Piper continued to plead.

Finally, Norah said in a testy voice, "Piper Carpenter, that is enough. I said no. Please go inside."

"Have you ever been? It's a lot of fun," Shane said.

"I... You're undermining my authority."

"What?" Shane chuckled.

"She needs to know that when I say no, I mean it, and begging will not make me change my mind."

"You didn't answer my question. Have you ever kayaked?"

"I've canoed. At summer camp."

He continued to chuckle. "How long ago was that?"

"None of your business! You'll be back next week?" she asked, and Shane nodded. Norah turned to follow Piper inside.

"It's a beautiful lake. You don't know what you're missing," he said.

Norah found Piper pouting in the kitchen. "Why couldn't we go with Shane? I love going to the lake, and we've only been twice this summer. I could have played longer with Gibbs."

"There are things that need to be done at home."

"Like what?"

"That's enough. The floors need to be washed, and there's laundry to do. You need to find something to do."

Piper walked away with a petulant look on her face and flopped onto the floor to play with her barn and stable. As she moved the animals around, she talked to them. "There was a dog named Gibbs here yesterday and today. I liked him. Yes, the barn and stable need a dog, but Mommy won't let me get one. She doesn't let me do anything fun."

Norah stood in the kitchen, rubbing her forehead. *She needs to learn life can't be fun and games all the time. Sam would have taken her to the lake.* As she had many times since she'd left him, Norah felt inadequate as a parent. *It's Shane being here, planting ideas in her head. At least four more weekends with him here. He has wrecked my whole routine.*

After Piper went to bed, Norah searched for tutorials on braiding hair. She studied techniques for French braids, pigtails, and buns. *I'll be damned if I let Sam be better at doing her hair than I am.* The next day, she stopped at the drugstore to buy hair ties, ribbons, and combs.

"I have a surprise for you," she said after dinner on Wednesday night.

Piper clapped her hands. "A dog?"

Norah's heart sank. Since Norah had picked her up, Piper had talked nonstop about Gibbs and how much she wanted a dog. "No." She handed Piper the bag from Monday.

"What are we going to do with all of this?" Piper laid everything out on the table, fingering the ribbons. "They're pretty. Am I going to take them to Daddy's?"

"No." Norah forced a smile. "I'm going to start doing your hair like Daddy does. We're going to practice tonight."

Piper looked dubious, but she sat quietly in the chair while Norah brushed her hair, until she hit a tangle. "Ouch! That hurts!" She pulled away.

"I must get the knots out first. I'll try to be gentle."

"Daddy says the same thing. I hate having my hair brushed."

Norah gave her the handheld mirror she'd purchased and brought up the videos she'd saved. "Let's start with pigtails."

After the pigtails, she and Piper watched the videos, and Piper selected an elaborate braid that she wanted Norah to do. They laughed as Norah fumbled and started over more than once. Finally, Piper declared it perfect, and Norah told her the last thing she wanted to do was the bun she needed for dance.

"I hate the bun. It hurts when Daddy pulls it tight."

"I know, but I heard you tell Shane you can't have any loose hairs. Let me try it."

Norah did her best to follow the instructions from the video, which had given tips on how to make the bun painless. She knew she was succeeding when Piper didn't make a sound as she worked. Piper admired the bun from all angles.

Then Norah opened the last bag. "You don't have to always have it in a ponytail or pigtails or braids. I bought these headbands. Your hair would look nice down, and these will keep it out of your face."

Norah tried several of them, and Piper clapped her hands. "I love them." She hopped out of the chair and hugged Norah. "This was fun."

Norah's heart filled. "It was. I still need more practice, though. Are you excited to see your dad and Sophie this weekend?"

"Yes! Do you think they had fun?"

"I imagine they did. And now you need to go to bed."

All right. I finally did something right. Norah looked at the weather app on her phone and decided they would have a picnic at the lake the next day. She wouldn't see Piper for five days after that, and she wanted to scour away the thought that Norah never let her have any fun.

Chapter Fourteen

Paddles and Possibilities

Shane

As Shane paddled around the lake after leaving Norah's house, he thought about another of Marcia's quotes, this one from J. P. Morgan: "A man always has two reasons for the things he does—a good one and the real one."

He snickered. *It's a blurry line between my reasons.* He thought about Piper and how much she enjoyed playing with Gibbs. "She tired you out, didn't she?" Gibbs sprawled on the front of the kayak, nearly asleep, instead of sitting up and observing the surroundings. "But man, her mother is something else. She's about the most tight-assed bitch I've ever met. And we both know I've met some bitches in my time." He chuckled. "How can she choose housework over being out here?"

He looked around. *This is quickly becoming my favorite lake.*

Four days later, Shane launched his kayak from the now-familiar beach and drank in the quiet of his surroundings. The buzz from the weekend crowds was gone, and the only noisy spot was at the north end, where the camp was. They were nearly back at the beach when Gibbs's tail started wagging. Shane raised his hand over his eyes, trying to shield them from the sun in the western sky.

Oh, I see what he's excited about. Piper was building a sandcastle on the edge of the water. Concentrating deeply on her work, she didn't see Shane approaching until Gibbs barked. Her head bobbed up.

She jumped up and started waving at Shane and Gibbs. "Mommy, it's Shane. He's out there with his kayak!"

Norah, sitting in a sand chair, put down the book she'd been reading. She waved with markedly less enthusiasm than her daughter. Gibbs's whole body shook with excitement as they got closer to the shore, and when Shane gave him the go-ahead, he jumped into the water and rushed to Piper's side. They rolled in the sand as Shane pulled the kayak onto dry land and walked over to Norah.

"Nice evening to be at the beach." Shane tried unsuccessfully to keep his eyes on her face. She was wearing a black tank suit, and he wished it were a bikini. "I didn't expect to see you here."

"We're having a picnic. Piper is going to her dad's for the weekend, so she won't be with me again until next Wednesday. I figured we should have a little fun." Her eyes challenged Shane. He couldn't determine if she was happy to see him or not.

"I brought my dinner as well." He retrieved his bag and sat on the sand next to Norah without bothering to ask if it was okay. He took out a sandwich and poured some water into a bowl for Gibbs.

"Pip, come here," Norah said. "We'll eat our dinner, and then you can play a little longer. Gibbs needs a drink of water."

As she ate, Piper said, "I've never seen a dog wear a life jacket. I wear one when I paddleboard, even though I know how to swim." Her tone made it obvious she wasn't a fan of the life vest.

"Gibbs can swim, but if we were to capsize, it would be a shock to his system, and he might forget how. Or he could get hit on the head and knocked out." He removed the vest and set it down. "This keeps him safe. You wear one for the same reason. Gibbs is the most important thing in my life, and I imagine your mom and dad feel the same way about you." He smiled at Piper and then turned his smile cautiously toward Norah.

She rewarded him with a smile.

When Piper went back to her sandcastle, Shane asked softly, making sure that Piper couldn't hear him, "Can I take her out in the kayak? I have a kid-sized vest in my truck."

Norah thought for a few minutes. "Yes, that's okay, but I want to leave in an hour." She cocked her head. "Do you have children?"

"No. However I have friends with kids, and they enjoy going out with me. Are you okay keeping track of Gibbs while we're on the water?"

She nodded. "Piper, would you like to go out on the water with Shane? In his kayak?"

"Yes!" She jumped up and walked back to Norah. "Really?"

"Really. He has a life jacket for you."

Shane steered the kayak across the south end of the lake then turned north, nervous about having his back to Norah and hoping Gibbs was okay with her. Piper kept up constant chatter, telling him about paddleboarding and asking questions. They cut across the lake and turned south to return to the beach. Piper waved wildly at Norah, and Shane was relieved to see his dog lying calmly at her feet. When they were almost back to shore, Shane jumped out, lifted Piper off the boat, and carried her to Norah.

"That was so fun! Thank you!" Piper was effusive in her thanks while she petted Gibbs, who had remained on the sand in front of Norah. "Can we go again sometime?"

"That will be up to your mom." He looked at Norah and got a noncommittal glance in return. "But I always have my kayak with me, so maybe it will work out again."

Leaving Piper and Norah on the beach, he loaded his kayak and paddles, packed up his dinner garbage, and got back in the car with Gibbs. "That was a pleasant surprise," he said to Gibbs as he drove home. "It's not every day that you get to lie at the feet of a pretty lady like her. I sense a tiny bit of a thaw." He couldn't deny the attraction he felt toward her.

Saturday morning, he knocked on Norah's door with a sense of anticipation. He'd loaded both kayaks into his truck, hoping Norah would be receptive to an invitation to go to the lake when he finished work for the day. His project was going well, and he was in a good mood. He expected Piper to come bounding out, but Norah was alone when she opened the door.

"I already unlatched the bulkhead so you can get in."

Wow. Her tone was markedly different from how it had been Thursday night. "Where's Piper? Gibbs is looking forward to seeing her."

"I told you, she's at her dad's this weekend."

"Damn. That's right, you did. Sorry, I forgot. I'll get to work." He could feel Norah's eyes on him as he unloaded the material from the truck and wondered if she felt any attraction to him. *If she does, she hides it very well.*

Sunday afternoon, after working at Norah's house, he packed his tools into the truck then went back to get Gibbs. Norah had made herself scarce for the two days, and he wouldn't risk rejection by inviting her to go kayaking. The friendliness he'd felt at the lake had evaporated, and he had no idea why.

Norah walked out to the truck as he started it. She signaled for him to roll down his window. "Could you leave Gibbs at home next weekend? All Piper has done since she met him is beg for a dog. If you don't bring him, maybe she'll stop."

"No." Shane looked at her incredulously. "Gibbs goes where I go. That's nonnegotiable." He shook his head. "Maybe you should think about all the ways that your daughter could benefit from having a dog instead of worrying about whether your floors are clean." Without waiting for a reply, he rolled up his window and roared out of the driveway. "Jesus. She's got some nerve. Wanting me to leave you at home. It doesn't matter how pretty she is—I need to put her out of my mind."

Midweek, Shane was still fuming about Norah's request that he leave Gibbs at home, when his phone rang with a call from Marcia.

"Hello," he said.

"Hey, my favorite client. We need to get our asses to Hollywood." Her excitement came through loud and clear.

"No!" His heartbeat sped up.

133

"Yes indeed. We have meetings scheduled for Friday and Saturday. If all goes well, you'll be signing the contract before we come home. Our flight leaves at noon tomorrow."

"That's unreal." His heart was pounding. "The group you've been talking to?"

"Yes. I'll meet you at the Admiral's Lounge in Terminal B."

Holy shit. Shane stood with his phone in his hand. This was one of his stretch goals, and he hadn't expected to reach it. *Not with the way I left.* He took a suitcase out of his closet and, looking at his clothes, debated what persona to present. Should he be a free-spirited creative or a buttoned-up businessman? Because no matter how creative he was, it was, after all, still a business.

He packed a variety of clothes and called his next-door neighbor to let him know Gibbs needed a place to stay. They chatted for a few minutes, and Shane said he would bring the dog over after dinner. Gibbs stood close by, looking at the suitcase.

"You know it means I'm leaving, but it also means you get to spend a few days with Keenan and Kasey." He was thankful for his neighbors and their sons, who loved Gibbs almost as much as he did, and for their reciprocal arrangement. Shane was happy to care for their dog when they traveled because they did the same for him.

Gibbs was safely delivered, Shane's bag was packed, and he had just one more thing to do before he went to bed. He stared at Norah's name on his phone, knowing he needed to make the call but hesitant about what her reaction would be. *I could text, but that would be the coward's way out.* Shane had never thought of himself as a coward. He punched the number and waited while it rang. *Maybe it'll go to voicemail and I can leave a message.*

"Hello." Her voice was tentative, the same as it had been when he'd returned her first call.

"Hey. I'm calling because I'm going out of town and won't be there this weekend. I'll be back next Saturday."

Her sigh was impossible to miss. "Is this because I asked you not to bring Gibbs? Are you punishing me?"

"No. I'm not that petty."

"Are you even going to come back to finish the job?"

"I said I'd be back next Saturday, and I will be." He hung up without saying goodbye, shaking his head.

Someone somewhere must have treated her very badly, because she is the least trusting woman I've ever met. He thought for a minute. *Not sure* trusting *is the right word, but she certainly hasn't succumbed to my charms.* He wasn't accustomed to being so thoroughly rejected.

Marcia stood to greet him when he entered the lounge, and he kissed her cheek. He was wearing khaki slacks, a blue button-up shirt, and a tweed sports coat.

Marcia's eyes signaled her approval. "You look nice."

"I opted for professional this trip." He grinned at her. "Although I have board shorts and T-shirts in my bag. If things go south, I can change my look. I knew when you mentioned the Admiral's Club that we'd be flying first class." He plucked a piece of cheese and a cracker off Marcia's plate. "This on my dime?"

"No. It's all on the producers. And they're putting us up in the Beverly Hills Hotel."

Shane raised his eyebrows. "Fancy." He filled a plate from the buffet table and picked up a bottle of water.

Marcia raised her glass toward him. "Water? Don't you want to celebrate?"

He knew she was drinking a vodka martini. "I'll have something after we board."

The flight attendant took their drink orders as they passed her on the way to their seats. While the passengers in coach were boarding, she handed Shane an old-fashioned.

He touched his glass to Marcia's. "Cheers."

"To lucrative contracts." She swallowed. "How are you feeling?"

"I'm excited. Cautiously excited." He contemplated his glass. "They know it's me?"

"Steve does. He's the one who pulled the team together."

"And that I do not want my name in any way affiliated with the film? Only my pen name is to be used."

"He's already signed the nondisclosure agreement. If he breaks the NDA, you'll be an even richer man than you are now."

"You've been working hard." Shane relaxed in his seat.

"Just trying to keep up with you. But if you sign on as the screenwriter, that will be as Shane Hilliker." Marcia met his eyes, daring him to challenge her.

"You're a lot surer of this move than I am."

"Stop it. You deserve to get the accolades. And do you know how rare it is for an author to write the screenplay?"

"I do." He sighed, shaking his head. "I do. It's been a long time since I've done any screenwriting."

"Twelve years." Marcia opened the book in her lap, leaving Shane to go back to the twenty-eight-year-old he'd been.

Shane

SHANE HILLIKER HAD BEEN a prodigy. People referred to his
father as the "plumber to the stars." His trade allowed him to
provide a comfortable life for his family, but he vehemently
opposed seeing Shane and his siblings—one brother and one
sister—grow up like the spoiled, entitled brats who ran rampant
through Los Angeles. They started working with him at a young
age, fetching tools and eventually learning the skills. His brother
and sister tired of the work and found jobs they liked better,
but Shane worked diligently with his father, and by the time
he started college, he could work on his own. He supported

himself while attending UCLA, graduated magna cum laude in three years, and enrolled at the Iowa Writers' Workshop graduate program. At twenty-three, master's degree in hand, he returned to California, determined to forge a career in television or movies. His first job was as a writer on *NCIS*. He spent two years there—a time so happy that, a dozen years later, when he got a dog, he quickly decided to name him after the lead on the show.

As happy as he'd been, when a new show beckoned, with a larger role for Shane, he jumped at the chance. The show was an instant success, and at twenty-six, he won an Emmy Award for writing. Suddenly, he was a hot commodity, with people clamoring for his talents. But as perfect as his life appeared, his departure from *NCIS* had started a three-year downward spiral.

Shane glanced at Marcia, who had fallen asleep and thought of the quote from Julia Child that he'd woken up to. "Drama is very important in life: You have to come on with a bang." *I went through that period with more than a bang.*

A flight attendant took his empty glass, and he nodded to let her know he'd like another. When it arrived, he took a long swallow and felt the warmth of the bourbon all the way down his throat. Alisha's death had been the first ding in his perfect life. She'd been a friend—occasionally, one with benefits. That night at the bar, Shane was so engrossed in conversation with a producer that he didn't notice how much she drank and let her leave without saying goodbye. Her death wrecked him, and he was disgusted with himself but not enough to make changes. The self-indulgent lifestyle his father had fought to protect him from sank its talons into Shane. He believed the praise that was heaped upon him, enjoyed the company of attractive women who thought he was the key to their big break, and bounced from one debauched night to the next. One Emmy became two, and his ego grew to match. Disagreements with his fellow writers became heated, with Shane refusing to back down even when he knew someone else had a better idea.

Twelve years ago, the day after Shane's twenty-eighth birthday, the newest writer on the team made a proposal that everyone but Shane loved. Truthfully, he loved it, too, but he couldn't admit it. Hungover, perhaps even still drunk from his celebration the night before, he ridiculed the writer. Unlike the veteran team members, who were accustomed to Shane's mockery, the young writer challenged him. The verbal sparring match escalated until the men stood, and after being shoved, Shane threw a punch that shattered the other man's jaw. The next morning, Shane was fired and given half an hour to gather his belongings. He'd never been in a fistfight, and he hunkered down in his house for several days, trying and failing to rationalize his behavior.

On the fifth day, his sister called. "How's every little thing?"

He knew instantly that she'd heard what had happened. That meant his parents and his brother also knew. He'd foolishly hoped he could keep it a secret. Despite its size, LA could be like a small town, and news traveled fast, especially when it involved everyone's favorite writer slugging a boy wonder.

"I'm fine. How about you?" He said a silent prayer that he was wrong about what she knew.

"That's not what I heard. My sources are surprised it hasn't happened before. What are you going to do now?"

"Find another gig. There are plenty of shows that need talented writers."

After several weeks, Shane realized a new writing job was not going to materialize. During a visit with his parents, his father said, "Heard you got knocked down a peg." This had been one of his favorite phrases when Shane was growing up.

Shane felt chagrined. "Maybe more than a peg."

"Hate to tell you this, but we all saw it coming."

"Would have been nice if someone had told me I'd become a douchebag."

His father raised his eyebrows. "Would you have listened?"

Shane slumped. The man had a point.

"Plenty of plumbing work available," his father said.

After two years of working in flooded basements and unclogging toilets, he had applied to the Bread Loaf Writers' Conference at Middlebury College. The ten days he spent there brought him back to life. He returned to LA, where the weather veered from drought to torrential downpours and from raging wildfires to catastrophic mudslides. The following summer, he returned to Vermont for the Bread Loaf Environmental Writers'

Conference. That week provided the fertilizer to germinate a seed Shane had been trying to grow for several months. He was going to write a novel that would highlight the devastating effects of climate change. He went home with an outline and the first five chapters written. Ten days later, after working on little sleep and a steady diet of caffeine and delivery from a burger joint, he had a rough draft for *Beneath the Burning Sky*. It would become the first book in his series the Fading Earth Chronicles.

Shane knew in his bones that this book would be a winner, and he didn't want it tainted by his name. He was determined not to be known as "best-selling author Shane Hilliker, who, by the way, broke a fellow writer's jaw not so long ago." So Hilton Shaw was born. Shane refused to have his picture or any personal information on the book jacket. He did no publicity, even though, when *Burning Sky* hit number one on the bestseller list, podcasters started clamoring for him to come on. He created a persona for Hilton, a fifty-five-year-old former oil-company executive appalled at having been part of the industry that had done such damage to the environment and to geopolitical relationships around the world. Hilton was a recluse who refused to disclose any personal details, including information about his family or where he lived. He released a book in the series every nine months and readers begged for the next one.

The only person who knew Hilton's true identity was Marcia. Shane had met her in a movie-business course at UCLA. They'd become best friends and maintained that friendship even when Marcia fled to New York City after her short-lived and disastrous marriage to an actor. She'd worked as an editor until she fell in love with Amelia, a medical researcher based in Boston. Marcia had moved in with Amelia and started her own firm, offering services to authors. She didn't sever her ties to Hollywood and always sought opportunities for her authors to ink movie deals. Shane had sent her his rough draft, and she'd been by his side ever since.

Three years earlier, wildfires had devastated his neighborhood, and while Shane didn't lose his house, he had had enough of LA and relocated to Vermont. The state had beckoned since he'd been at Bread Loaf. For the first time in his life, he didn't feel on edge. He developed friendships and bought a kayak for long paddles on the water, where he worked out plot points. In the winter, he exchanged snowshoes for the kayak, and he stopped being tethered to his phone. Most importantly, he kept plumbing tools in his truck to remind him of his roots. He volunteered for Habitat for Humanity and helped friends when they had leaking pipes. Life was good.

Marcia's eyes fluttered open. "Sorry about that. I was up late last night, saying goodbye to Amelia." She grinned at Shane.

"I'm surprised she isn't traveling with us."

"She couldn't get away from work. But she'll fly out tomorrow night. It's not every day that I stay at the Beverly Hills Hotel. I couldn't pass up having some time there with Amelia."

"Steve's the first person you've revealed Hilton's identity to. I appreciate how diligently you've guarded my privacy."

"I know. It means a lot that you trust me with it."

Shane squeezed her hand. "Still not sure how I feel about being the screenwriter. Hollywood has a long memory."

She scoffed. "Over the last twelve years, there has been a lot of behavior much more egregious than yours. We'll listen to what they have to say and then decide." The flight attendant brought them food and refreshed Marcia's drink. "How's Hildy?"

Shane guffawed. "She's great. Three chapters left to write in *Love, Lies and Lethal Secrets*." He laughed again.

Marcia shook her head. "Only you would start another series in a totally different genre and skyrocket to the top of the best-seller list."

"What can I say? I'm a talented writer."

"With such a small ego." Banter was easy between the two of them, something Shane appreciated. "I worry that representing two authors who keep their identities totally locked down is going to raise eyebrows."

"Come on. Hildy's an open book." As Shane had settled into the leisurely pace that life in Vermont presented, he'd felt the need to write something less heavy than the Fading Earth Chronicles. He settled on a cozy mystery featuring a bickering married couple, Miles and Millicent Holt. That book, *Blissfully Bewitched*, streaked to number one, and Shane had so much fun writing it that he made it a series, and Married to Mystery was born. Readers fell in love with Miles and Millicent, as well as their creator, Hildy Shackleton.

A friend helped Shane create a portrait of Hildy, which appeared on the book covers. A twenty-seven-year-old female, she suffered from severe anxiety and agoraphobia. She refused to do live interviews but would submit answers to questions for print interviews. She was selective about which requests she accepted, and she maintained almost as large an air of mystery as Hilton did.

"Three magazine interviews do not equal an open book," Marcia said.

"Maybe she'll do another one next year."

"I could do so much if you'd let me get the real you out there." This was an ongoing discussion between them. When Shane shook his head, Marcia sighed. "This book came together more quickly than you expected. Lots of long paddles feeding your muse?"

Shane rolled his shoulders. "Somewhat, but I'm working on a plumbing job too." Solitary endeavors helped him work out plot points.

"Another Habitat project?"

"No." He chuckled. "Someone steered me to a damsel in distress with no hot water. Her plumbing is a mess, and after some back-and-forth, she hired me to give it a makeover."

"Hired?"

"I'm using the word loosely. I don't want to take her money, but she's fairly insistent. It's all going to Habitat."

"I'd expect nothing less. Have you worked your charms on her?"

"She's made it very clear she doesn't find me charming."

"That's what you get for living in the sticks like a hermit. You've lost your touch."

"I've lost something. She's pretty but prickly, and no matter what I say, it's not the right thing."

Chapter Sixteen

Thetford on a Tuesday Night

Shane

SHANE STOOD IN FRONT of the mirror and slid the knot on his tie into place, confident that dressing as a professional was the right choice. He chuckled, remembering Marcia's voicemail from Mark Twain. "Clothes make the man. Naked people have no influence in society." A free-spirited-creative style would have resurrected echoes of the twenty-eight-year-old asshole who'd broken a coworker's jaw. He was uncharacteristically nervous. Financially, he didn't need to make this deal, but emotionally—that was another matter. He glanced around the room. There was no denying that he and Marcia were being treated like VIPs. They had a car and driver waiting to do their bidding, and the hotel was magnificent. Hotel staff had assigned them deluxe rooms, one with a balcony and one with a patio. Shane deferred to Marcia, who'd chosen the patio. He was glad she'd get to spend time with Amelia. This deal had been in the works for more than six months, and Marcia deserved some relaxation.

The room's pastel shades gave it a relaxing vibe, making it feel like an oasis in the city. After dinner the night before, Shane had poured a shot of bourbon and gone out to the balcony to enjoy it. He looked out at gardens and palm trees and felt a pang of jealousy for Marcia and Amelia. It would be nice to have a woman to share this with. Over a second shot, his thoughts went to Norah. He liked her, prickly personality and all. Maybe when he got home, he'd put more effort into wooing her.

He and Marcia left for the meeting. Their driver navigated the notorious Los Angeles traffic, and Shane remembered all the reasons he preferred his life in Vermont.

In the elevator to the top floor, Marcia asked, "Nervous?"

"Truthfully? A little."

"Remember, they approached me. They want your stories."

Shane looked around the table as they entered the room, recognizing only one individual. He extended his hand. "Hey, Steve. It's good to see you."

They'd worked together on *NCIS*, and Shane had believed, from the beginning of Marcia's negotiations, that Steve had to be the force behind this project.

Steve grabbed Shane's hand. "It's been a long time. Let me introduce everyone." He went around the table, naming the two women and two men who formed his team. A couple of the names were familiar to Shane, and the others were complete strangers.

Three hours later, they left the building. Marcia broke into a huge smile. "That went even better than I hoped for."

"It went well," Shane agreed.

"You're allowed to be excited."

"I know. It's surreal being here."

Back at the hotel, they went to Marcia's patio and reviewed every detail of the contract. He would have six months to write the screenplay and three months for revisions. If all went as planned, the movie would premiere at Christmas in two and a half years.

"The timeline boggles my mind. We worked so much faster in television," he said.

"Will you do the screenplay?"

"Yeah." He rewarded her with a wide smile. "I like the idea. And it won't have a tremendous impact on my other writing either. You were amazing, talking about Hilton and what a recluse he is. I was cracking up inside."

"That's what you pay me for. We'll meet with the group Steve has lined up for tomorrow—tell them we agree in principle but need to have our legal team review it. And of course, I must convince Hilton to go along with it." She smiled at Shane. "I have one more surprise for you. A streaming service approached me about making Married to Mystery into a series. I have meetings on Monday. That's why we're not flying back until Tuesday."

"When did that happen?"

"The initial call came a few weeks ago. I let them know I was coming to town, and we nailed down the schedule."

"Are you going to get me the screenwriting gig for that too?" he asked.

"Do you want that? Because it would mean spending a lot of time here."

"It would. Take the meetings, and we can discuss it."

Shane, Marcia, and Amelia toasted with champagne on the return flight. The contract was on its way to the lawyer, and Shane would travel to Boston to meet with her the following week. He sat across the aisle from the women and watched the affectionate gestures between them. He'd never had that type of relationship—never been in love, if he was honest with himself. Putting himself back into the world he'd abandoned was a big step. Maybe it was time to take another big step and get more serious about finding a partner.

On a whim, he took a route home that led him through Thetford. The sun was setting as he turned into Norah's driveway. He strode to her door and knocked firmly.

Norah's face appeared in the window, and seconds later, she opened the door but left the screen door closed, a barrier between them. "Shane, what are you doing here?" She was wearing yellow satin shorts and a tank top with a sunflower on it. Her hair was piled on top of her head.

"I want you to understand that when I say I'm going to do something, I follow through." He placed his hand on the screen-door handle but found it locked. "Can I come in?"

"Why?"

"Because I don't like the tension between us. I feel like no matter what I say, I offend you somehow. That's not a typical reaction. I get along well with most people."

"Most *female* people because they're dazzled by your good looks?"

He tried to hide his smile as he shrugged. "Whatever you say. Are you going to let me in? I want to clear the air before the weekend. When I'll be back. As I promised."

Slowly, her hand moved to the lock, and she opened the door. "Where have you been? That's formal attire for a Tuesday night in Thetford."

He paused, unsure how much he wanted to disclose. "I was in California for some business meetings. It's easier to travel in these clothes than to pack them." He stepped into the house and stopped in front of Norah.

"Were you doing this... or that?" she asked.

Shane cocked his head.

"You still haven't told me what you do, other than 'this and that,'" she explained.

"It was a little of both. It pissed me off when you asked me not to bring Gibbs, and I reacted badly. I want to apologize. I'm sure you have good reasons for not having pets."

Norah scratched the back of her head and looked around before letting her gaze return to Shane. "I don't. Other than I think an animal in the house would be a lot of work. Walks for a dog, picking up dog poo in the yard." A slight grin crossed her face. "I've watched you."

Shane grinned back.

Norah continued, "A cat would require a litter box, and either a dog or a cat would leave tons of hair everywhere. I like to keep my house clean."

"I've noticed."

"Piper doesn't have a pet at her dad's either." Her defensive tone was hard to miss.

"Is it a competition?"

"No!" She frowned. "Maybe a little... sometimes. Mostly, we coparent well."

"He's remarried, huh?" He watched for a reaction and saw none. "Piper told me."

"Sam and I weren't married. I don't believe in marriage."

"Obviously he does."

Her expression changed. "See, you say things like that, and I feel like they are digs at me."

"I don't mean it that way. I'll have to work on my filter. If I do that, can you work on not taking offense at everything I say?"

"I don't take offense at everything."

"Pretty close. And you still haven't accepted my apology."

She heaved a sigh. "I accept your apology. There, are you happy now?"

"Yes. Thank you." He smiled his most disarming smile.

Norah rewarded him with a smile of her own. "Are we good? I'll see you Saturday, with Gibbs?"

"Yes." He held her in his gaze.

Norah didn't shy away, keeping her eyes locked on his. "Is there anything else?"

"Yes." Shane leaned down, bringing his lips to hers—softly at first, half expecting her to slap his face.

When she didn't, he intensified the pressure and took a step closer to her. He embraced her. She was small against his solid body and smelled like jasmine. Her lips moved against his, and the fascination he'd been fighting since the first day was amped up. As the kiss went on, she moved her hands to his hips, and it was hard to hide his developing erection.

He dropped his arms and moved toward the door. "Tell me to leave."

"No."

"Is Pip here?" He knew where he hoped this would go, and he would not do that with a child in the house. "Do you mind my calling her Pip?"

"She's at Sam's on Monday and Tuesday." She closed the distance he'd created between them. "And Pip is fine." She caressed his cheek. "Kiss me again."

Norah's fingers on his face lit a fire, and Shane struggled to curb the want that washed over him. He reached for the top of her head and gently removed the hair tie. With an easy flick of his fingers, it joined the red one he always had on his wrist. He fluffed her hair, buried his face in it, and inhaled deeply.

"Jasmine surrounds my parents' house. This scent takes me home." His hands moved to her face, and he lowered his lips to hers again. Her lips parted, and he recognized the invitation. His tongue plunged into her mouth and explored, tangling with hers.

Norah moved back and bumped against the wall. Shane didn't sense that she was trying to get away, but he wanted to be sure. He broke the kiss and looked at her with a question in his eyes. She took his hand and led him into the house. Shane kicked the door closed as they walked away from it. He expected to land in the living room, but instead, they walked down a small hall to her bedroom. The erection that had started when he saw her in the yellow shorts was now threatening to burst out of his pants.

Norah grasped his sport coat and attempted to move it past his shoulders. Shane shrugged it off and threw it into a corner. She undid the top button on his shirt and fumbled with the next one. Then she stopped fumbling, gripped each side of the shirt, and tugged, popping off all the buttons.

"I'll buy you a new one," she murmured.

Shane could hardly breathe. "No need." He tossed the shirt on top of his jacket, and as Norah brought her hands to his abs, he closed his eyes. Her touch was magical.

"Turn around," she said.

"What?" Shane wasn't sure what Norah was asking.

"I want to see that tattoo on your back."

He slowly turned, and shivered as Norah traced the book titles, which included the first book Shane could remember reading on his own, *Dinosaurs in the Dark* from the Magic Treehouse series. Books that had affected him, from grade school through college and everyday life, completed the tattoo of a tornado erupting from an open book. He'd had it done the winter after he moved to Vermont. At the top of the tornado was *Beneath the Burning Sky*, his first published novel.

Norah's fingers moved down his back to the waistband of his pants, and he turned to face her. Shane reached for her tank top and fingered the satin material. He let his hand drift to the hem and, after silently checking with her, tugged it over her head. Her breasts were small and perfect. He traced the tan line from her bathing suit then lowered his mouth to her breasts. He teased the nipples, relishing the way they responded. This kind of restraint was not his usual approach, but he was leery of doing anything that might scare her away. What he really wanted to do was throw her onto the bed and show her how much he wanted her.

She stepped toward him, an arm out to touch his hair the way he had touched hers. Her bare chest came to his, and both of them trembled. She reached for his belt buckle.

"Wait." Shane held her hand. "Protection?"

Chapter Seventeen

Playing With Passion

Norah

SHE ROLLED HER EYES. "Birth control isn't an issue." She shook her hand free and returned to his belt. "And I'm clean." She'd had a yearly exam two months earlier, which included testing.

Shane squirmed. "I honestly don't know about me."

Norah's face fell. "I don't have anything."

"Me either." He drew her back to him and kissed her again, letting all his desire surface. "We can play." He fluttered kisses down her neck, taking a breast into his mouth, causing a quiver Norah couldn't hide. "I'm good at playing."

She wanted to have sex—that last time with Tom had been months ago—but she appreciated Shane's honesty. *Let's see what he's got.* If the rest of him matched his chest and shoulders, she knew she'd be impressed. *And I'm not faking anything tonight.*

"Okay," she murmured then tugged on his pants again. "Do you keep these on when you're playing?"

"No." He chuckled as he unbuckled his belt and pushed the pants to the floor. "Now you." He reached for the satin shorts, fingered the material the same way he had her top, and slid them down her legs. His hands ran down her sides, over her slim waist, to her softly rounded hips. "You're beautiful. And I want to explore every inch."

He sank to the bed and pulled her into his lap. His erection was obvious through his boxers, and Norah willed herself to relax. His mouth was performing a symphony on her breasts, and she knew the depth of her desire was obvious. She groaned as he moved a hand between her legs. If he didn't already know how aroused she was, he would when he felt her wetness. She searched for something to do, but his mouth was busy, and she couldn't reach any of his body parts. All she could do was sit on his lap with his erection beneath her while he played.

Shane gently pushed her to the mattress and lay beside her. He alternated between kisses that took away what breath she had left and attention to her breasts. His fingers found her clit and teased her to the brink of an orgasm. Norah reached for his boxers and found the substantial bulge, bringing a groan from Shane. His fingers slipped from her clit to inside, and she thrust against them.

Norah didn't know how long they continued like this, with Shane varying his speed and her stroking his erection. His fingers went back to her clit while he was still suckling her breast, and when he nipped the nub, she orgasmed noisily, unable to stay silent. Shane's erection grew as Norah shook with the strength of her climax.

As her heartbeat returned to normal, Norah's hand found its way into Shane's boxers. She gasped at the size of his erection and struggled in the small space between the cloth and his torso. She wanted to give him as much pleasure as he had given her.

"Can you take off the boxers?"

He shimmied out of them. "You don't have to ask me twice."

The movement of his hips and the sight of his cock brought Norah back to the brink of an orgasm. She gripped him and stroked from balls to tip, watching his face. His eyes were closed, and Norah increased her speed as his erection grew.

His breath was coming quickly, but he managed to spit out, "I like your breasts."

She stopped stroking, which earned her a groan from Shane, and he opened his eyes. Norah repositioned herself so his mouth could reach her breast and then resumed her attention to his erection.

Shane closed his eyes again and murmured, "Yes."

Norah watched his face contort as his orgasm hit. The sticky cum showered both of them, and she didn't care. She guided his hand back to her clit, and he expertly triggered another orgasm while still recovering from his. She lay next to him, gasping for air, as Shane held her. Her heartbeat had nearly slowed to normal when he climbed off the bed and walked toward the hall. She heard the water run in the bathroom, and a minute later, he returned with a washcloth and towel. When he finished wiping away the stickiness, he carefully dried her then lay back down, and she settled her head on his shoulder. He buried his face in her hair, and she could hear him inhaling the scent. His fascination charmed her.

"Do you want me to leave?" he asked.

"No. But I need to go back out to the living room and kitchen to turn out the lights. My neighbors will think something is wrong if they see the house all lit up in the middle of the night." She slipped off the bed and pulled on the shorts and tank top that were in a pile on the floor.

Shane followed her, sliding his boxers over his hips in a fluid motion. Norah walked to the kitchen, and Shane went to shut off the lamp near the love seat. His breath caught when he saw the book sprawled on the coffee table—*Echoes in the Ash*. It was the latest in his series. She'd been reading it when he knocked on her door.

As Norah joined him, he jutted his chin toward the book. "Have you read the entire series?"

"Yes. Have you? It's fantastic."

"I've read it all, and I liked it. I hate the damage we're doing to the environment. It's not as obvious here as it is in California."

"It may be more subtle, but it's here nonetheless." She picked up the book, inserted a bookmark, and placed it back on the table. "I work for the agency charged with implementing Vermont's climate initiatives. Did you know that?"

"I didn't. Some of those are controversial."

"Tell me about it." She shrugged. "Change is hard, and balancing costs and results is even more difficult." She took his hand and tugged him back toward the bedroom. "There's a rumor that *Echoes* may be Hilton's last book in the Chronicles."

Shane snickered. "Is the author a personal friend?"

"I wish." Norah chuckled. "When I find an author I like, I try to learn everything I can about them. I follow them on social media. Go to book signings. I've wasted so much time looking for information on Hilton Shaw, and there's nothing."

"He's a former oil company executive."

"See. You've searched too."

"Maybe a little."

Norah removed the decorative pillows from her bed and pulled the covers down. She pointed toward the far side. "You can have that side. This is mine."

Shane lay down with his arm extended over her pillow. "Come here." He ran his hand back and forth over the satin. "What time do you get up for work?"

"Actually, I'm taking tomorrow off. Piper and I are meeting some friends at the lake."

"Ahh, you're going to have some fun." His voice was thick with drowsiness. "Norah? This was fun."

Norah arrived at Sam's, and Piper tore out of the door and into her arms, just as she'd been doing since she started walking. Norah chatted with Sophie for a few minutes before gathering Piper for the drive to the lake.

"Where are Caitlin and Janey? Aren't they meeting us here?" Piper asked.

"Yes, but they have farther to drive than we do. We'll relax until they get here."

Piper splashed into the water, and Norah's eyes were on her, but her mind remained fixed on the previous night. Shane's appearance at her door had shocked her. She knew she'd offended him when she asked him not to bring Gibbs and then again on the telephone call, but she hadn't expected him to show up at her house without warning. His usual attire was a T-shirt and shorts or jeans, and seeing him dressed up took her breath away. He was ruggedly handsome, and his white shirt was stretched tightly over his chest. She fought the fire raging inside her throughout their conversation. All she wanted to do was run her hands over his chest and tangle her fingers in his hair. When he leaned in to kiss her—such a surprisingly gentle kiss—any hesitation she'd felt vanished. The idea of getting naked with him had been born on the first day, when he'd walked shirtless across her lawn. She found him bossy and presumptuous but also extraordinarily sexy.

He'd given her so many moments to stop it, asking if she wanted him to leave and whether Pip was home. He hadn't presumed that shortening her name was okay. Norah had been crushed when he admitted he wasn't sure about his health status. *Playing* wasn't what she'd wanted.

I wanted to have wild, uncontrolled sex. But oh my God, he wasn't kidding—he's very good at playing. Remembering the feel of Shane's mouth on her breast and his fingers on her clit brought back the same desire she'd felt the night before. *His timing was perfect. He didn't prolong the foreplay, and that first orgasm came so easily. He didn't presume that I wanted him to stay...*

Caitlin and Janey arrived while Norah was deep in thought. The two women went into the water with their daughters and stayed until all four of them were shivering. Then Piper and Janey settled at the edge of the lake to build a sandcastle. Caitlin set up a chair next to Norah's and reached into her bag for two wine coolers.

Norah opened hers. "I thought no alcohol while you're breastfeeding."

"That's true, but Matty decided about a month ago that he was through with Mama's milk. It was a couple of months earlier than I expected." She opened her bottle. "I weaned the other kids around their first birthdays, and he won't be one for another month."

"Are you sad?"

"Not really. I thought I would be, but I feel like I gave him a good start, and now I have my body back."

"You look great," Norah said.

"Thanks. Now that my chest isn't hampered by two huge milk jugs, it's easier to work out." Both women laughed. "That was my big news. What's new with you? I'm sorry the online dating didn't work out."

Shortly after Norah's spa day with Caitlin, she had set up a dating profile on a site that claimed it was for business executives. Willing to travel for an interesting match, she cast a wide geographic net.

"It was so bad, Cait. I expected college graduates climbing the corporate ladder. And instead, most of the matches seemed like someone I would meet at the Sidecar on a Saturday night. Flannel-wearing guys who barely made it through high school." Norah laughed. "I sound like a snob."

Cait grimaced. "A little. I thought it was an exclusive site."

"It was supposed to be. A couple of weeks after I canceled my membership, I found out the site had been hacked. By that time, I was tired of the whole thing. I'll either find someone organically, or I'll stay blissfully single. I don't think the type of man I'm looking for exists in Vermont."

"Are you still looking for someone that Mommy and Daddy will like?"

"No!"

"You say that, but your actions don't match up." Caitlin was Norah's only friend who made her face reality. "You write off a large portion of the population."

"I don't. I just want someone who's..." Norah didn't finish her thought.

Caitlin finished it for her. "Good enough for you? Mitzi and Bennet drummed that into all of you, and you're the only one who hasn't met their expectations."

Norah groaned. "We've had this conversation so many times. There must be something more interesting to talk about."

Caitlin shook her head. "I find your attempts to break free from your upbringing quite fascinating."

"I slept with my plumber last night." Norah had told her friend about her struggles to find someone to work on her plumbing and how she'd ended up with Shane. She'd described the hair and the tats and how much he exasperated her but not the desire he sparked.

"You *what?*" Caitlin shrieked, and the girls looked up from their sandcastle.

"Shush! This is between you and me."

"How did that happen?"

Norah described how she'd found Shane on her doorstep and the first tender kiss between them. "I melted. And then he asked me to tell him to leave. Do you know how huge that is? No guy ever does that. I led him to the bedroom and ripped his shirt off."

"Seriously?" Caitlin laughed. "That's not like you."

"I'd seen him shirtless once, from a distance, and I had to see that chest again. I started unbuttoning it, but that was taking too long, so I just..." Norah mimicked pulling on the sides of Shane's shirt.

Both women roared with laughter, and the girls ran up from the beach. "What's so funny?" they asked.

Caitlin recovered first. "I was telling Norah how you kids react to Matty's messy diapers."

Janey frowned. "That's not funny." She looked at Piper. "They're disgusting." She shuddered.

"It's funny to us moms," Norah said. "It looks like you have an entire village of sand buildings on the beach. We'll have lunch in an hour. You can go back in the water." The girls scurried off, and Norah continued describing her night. "He has a tattoo on his back that I had to see. It's a tornado of book titles. *Book titles,* Cait! And he reads Hilton Shaw!"

"Maybe there's more to the plumber than meets the eye."

"I don't know." Norah shrugged. "But last night was one for the books. The orgasms were great, but it was his kindness that got to me. His lack of presumption. He asked if I wanted him to leave, not if he could stay. It's a subtle difference, but it's huge."

"And is that all that was huge?" Caitlin chuckled.

"No." Norah giggled. "He's well-endowed. But back to the kindness. He asked if Pip was there before we'd gone very far, and if it was okay to call her Pip. He didn't ask if he could see me tonight or anything even close to that."

"You think it was one and done? Sounds like you'd like more."

"I would. Maybe I'll have to jump him."

"This is not typical Norah behavior."

"I know. Maybe because I sense it will be short-lived. Once he's done working at my house, I'll never see him again. It's not like we're in the same social circle."

"There you go again. You could expand your social circle." Caitlin sighed. "I love Jesse with all my heart, but the idea of a man appearing at my door at sunset to kiss his way into my bedroom is an epic fantasy. Thank you for letting me live vicariously through you and the tattooed plumber."

Chapter Eighteen
Connections

Shane

"'YOU CAN GET WHAT you want, or you can just get old.' That's from Billy Joel. Things are going well at this end. Our meeting with the lawyer is on Wednesday."

Shane had finished *Love, Lies, and Lethal Secrets* and was going over the manuscript before he sent it off for line editing. Marcia had sent him several questions, and he'd answered them all.

On Friday, he and Gibbs had gone to a lake near the Canadian border and spent the entire day there. Typically, when he kayaked, Shane worked out plot points, but as his paddle cut through the serene water, he wasn't thinking as Hilton Shaw or Hildy Shackleton. And he didn't think about the screenplay he'd be working on in a matter of weeks. He thought about the night with Norah.

He hadn't intended to kiss her when he stopped by. He'd wanted to clear the air. It was as simple as that. But the conversation went better than he'd anticipated. Her tone had never reverted to the icy one that he'd heard a couple of times.

It was the outline of her breasts under that satin. He'd been unable to resist. Her lips were sweet, and the jasmine scent of her hair had fed his desire. But all of that was minor. What really did him in was that she wanted him as much as he wanted her. He purposely gave her chances to stop, and she didn't. Her responsiveness fed his craving, and her orgasm came so easily. She didn't miss a beat making him come. When he murmured about liking her breasts, she changed position smoothly so his mouth could reach one. He fully expected her to want him to leave. Going to sleep with her nestled on his shoulder was the icing on the cupcake. Or so he thought until he awoke when she left the bed. He listened to her walk to the bathroom, heard the water run, and pretended to be asleep when she climbed back into bed.

She whispered in his ear. "I know you're not asleep. I want to play some more." Her lips crashed against his, and she plunged her tongue into his mouth.

The jasmine, her words, and the kiss took his breath away. His hands glided along the satin of her top while she explored his mouth. Eventually, he shoved it up, and Norah tore it off. He let a breast fill one hand while his other snaked into her shorts. She was already wet, and he was already hard.

Her hand went to the bulge of his erection, and her touch through the jersey material was almost as hot as skin to skin. "There isn't room in there for my hand."

"It's okay—just do what you're doing." He didn't want to stop.

He fingered her clit, and she started thrusting against his hand. She made a mewing sound that captivated him, and their movements became more frantic until he felt her shudder with an orgasm at the exact moment he exploded. He clutched her tightly while their heartbeats returned to normal.

He'd relived it all while he paddled around the lake. And now it was Saturday morning, and as he loaded his truck, he chuckled, thinking about Marcia's quote that morning. He knew what he wanted, but he had no idea if it would happen. She'd told him on the first day that she had Piper every other weekend, and he hadn't been there enough to know the schedule. Neither of them had mentioned a repeat performance when they parted in the morning. He'd taken a shower, put on his khakis and the shirt—minus the buttons—and carried his sport coat out to the kitchen. He thought her eyes lit up at the sight of him, but he wasn't sure.

She offered him a cup of coffee and told him she needed to leave to pick up Piper. "I'll see you on Saturday."

Shane had called his doctor on the way home and stopped at the hospital to have blood drawn. If there was going to be another encounter with Norah, it was going to be the full experience.

Piper rushed out of the house when he drove in. "Hi, Shane! Hi, Gibbs!"

Her excitement tickled him, and he let her lead Gibbs to the back lawn. Norah was watching from the deck, and Shane felt oddly shy about seeing her again.

He turned to face her, smiling. "Pip's a good dog wrangler. I appreciate the help."

"You and Gibbs being here today is all she's talked about since Wednesday."

"Did you have fun at the lake?"

"We had a lovely day. I unlocked the bulkhead for you." She disappeared inside, and Shane started working.

At the end of the day, he found two glasses of iced tea and a bowl of water waiting on the porch. He joined Norah at the small table, and she asked him about the work. He told her what he had completed.

"My status matches yours," he added.

Piper was on the lawn, throwing a ball with Gibbs. "What's a status?"

Norah grinned. "Kids hear everything."

"It's a word that can describe the condition of something. Last time I saw your mother, she said her refrigerator was a mess, and I was telling her mine is too."

Norah rolled her eyes and whispered, "My fridge is never a mess."

Shane smiled and shrugged.

"Are you going kayaking when you leave?" Piper asked.

"I am. And I should get going because it's getting dark earlier now." He wanted to invite them to join him but also wanted to be respectful of Norah's parenting boundaries.

"You've got two. Is someone else going with you?"

"I don't know." He looked at Norah, raised his eyebrows, and hoped his silent communication skills meshed with hers.

She mouthed, "Ask us."

"Would you and your mom like to come with Gibbs and me?"

"Can we? Please?" Piper hopped on one foot while she waited for Norah to answer.

"I think that sounds like fun."

They used both kayaks—Shane took Piper on his and let Gibbs ride with Norah. He kept them close to the shore, and when they returned to the beach, there was a food truck parked nearby.

"I'm going to get a sandwich. Do you want anything?" he asked.

"We get sandwiches there when I come here with Daddy and Sophie." Piper looked at Norah. "They're really good."

"Okay, let me get some money."

"I've got it."

Norah huffed. "You know I still haven't given you any money for the work you're doing."

"Hadn't really thought about it." He grinned and led them to the truck.

As they ate, Piper kept up a constant chatter. "Next week, I'm going to stay with Daddy because Mommy is going on a vacation with Aunt Betsy."

Shane gave Norah a questioning look.

"My sister," Norah said. "She lived near me until six months ago, when she fell in love and moved to Colorado. We miss each other, so we're taking a girls' trip to Italy."

This was the most personal information Norah had volunteered, and he felt a tinge of sadness that he wouldn't see her for such a lengthy period. His attraction to her was growing by leaps and bounds. "That sounds like fun for you and fun for Piper. Does next week mean tomorrow?"

Norah shook her head. "We leave a week from Monday. What's this week look like for you?"

"This and that." He smiled when Norah rolled her eyes. "I'm going to Boston on Wednesday to meet with my lawyer. How about you?"

"I have a meeting in Montpelier on Monday. I won't get home until five." She leaned over and pulled Piper's braid. "Good thing you're at your dad's that day." Her face told Shane everything he wanted to know.

Shane was sitting at the table on the porch, along with two iced coffees, when Norah arrived. As she climbed out of her car, he appreciated the view of her legs that her black pencil skirt gave him. She wore black high heels that enhanced her already shapely calves. Shane closed his eyes, trying to tamp down the desire that was building. When he opened them, she was standing in front of him. Her hair was in a severe knot on top of her head, and she wore a white silk blouse.

Oh, what I want to do with that silk.

"Hope you don't mind," he said. "You had iced coffee the other night at the lake. Thought you might like one today."

"Thank you." She joined him at the table. "It's a nice way to end the day."

Oh, honey, the day's just getting started. Shane took a deep breath.

"How did *this* go? Or was it *that* you worked on today?"

He grinned, happy to have her baiting him. "A little of both."

They sipped in silence for a few minutes. Then Norah stood. "Would you like to come in?"

He followed her in and shut the door behind him. He brought one hand around her back and let it slip from her shoulder to her waist. The silk felt rich.

"Come here." He wanted her to close the tiny distance between them.

She took a step forward and meshed her body against him, and it felt as good as it had the first time. He held her close with his other arm and felt her go up on tiptoe. Her mouth met his, and the fireworks began. Shane had controlled himself the previous week, but he wouldn't tonight—at least not this first time. And he quickly realized Norah wasn't holding back either. Her tongue plunged into his mouth, and her hands went around his neck. With a quick jump, she hooked her legs around his hips.

His hands settled under her butt and held her close. "Bedroom?"

"Unless you want to do it here," she teased.

Shane strode toward the bedroom, and bumped against the wall when Norah nibbled on his ear. He turned around and sat on the bed with her on his lap. They kissed hungrily until he drew back and started working the buttons on her blouse. They were tight, and it was taking longer than he'd expected.

"Do you want to tear it off like I did yours?"

"I'm considering it." He had four buttons undone. He reached for the hem. It passed easily over her head, and his breath caught at the sight of her lacy white bra. He caressed the lace, enjoying the shiver that went through her.

"Shane. I don't want to play tonight—not right now, anyway. I want to fuck."

He stood, placing her feet on the floor. "I can do that."

He unbuttoned her skirt and slid it over her hips. She was wearing white panties that matched the bra, and he shoved those to the floor. He unbuttoned his jeans and stepped out of them. Norah grasped his T-shirt, pulled it over his head, then moved her hands to the bulge in his boxers. Shane stripped them off, and his heartbeat increased as he watched her get a good look at his cock for the first time. She reached for the back of her bra, and Shane stopped her.

"No. Leave it on." He eased one breast out of the cup, lowered his mouth, and sucked hard, enjoying the mewing sounds coming from Norah.

Her hands caressed his abs, and finally, mercifully, she wrapped one around his erection. She sat on the edge of the bed, and he pushed her to the mattress. He continued to tease her breast while she stroked him.

One hand snuck between her legs. "You're wet."

"And you're hard. Let's bring those together."

He straddled her and brought the tip of his cock to her clit then eased it in. Her hips rose to meet him as she took his length.

He plunged into her, trying to go slowly, but his thrusts quickly became frenzied. As he felt his orgasm rising, he slipped his fingers against her clit, remembering how responsive she'd been to that the week before. He felt her come, and he let go with a shout. Then, not wanting to crush her, he rolled to the side and pulled her tightly against him. They lay silently until their breathing returned to normal.

Shane brought his lips back to hers. "You have the sweetest lips." He continued kissing her for several minutes then rose up on his elbow so he could see her. He tucked her breast back into the bra and fondled the lace again. "That was great. Was it for you?"

"Yes. And that's not always true for me. Thank you."

He hugged her again, enjoying the way she relaxed against him. "Thanks for sharing that with me."

"Tell me about your tattoos."

"The one on my back is books that affected me. I like to read. The sleeve is a jumble. Places I've traveled to, a couple of quotes, and a boyhood dog. I started it when I was eighteen and added to it over the years. The tornado was more well thought-out. How about you? Any ink?"

"No." Her tone made it clear the idea of a tattoo had never crossed her mind. "Are you hungry? There's a restaurant I like that delivers."

"Are you inviting me to stay for dinner?"

"I'm hoping you'll stay all night."

"I'd like that."

"Where's Gibbs?"

"He stays with my neighbors when I'm away overnight," he said. She was being very blunt with him, and he decided he could do the same. "I was hoping to stay, and I wasn't sure how you'd feel about me bringing Gibbs."

"You can bring him tomorrow night."

"Nope. If I stay here tomorrow, I'll be heading directly to Boston the next morning."

"On the weekend, then. Pip won't be here. You can stay overnight. And Gibbs can too." When Shane didn't respond, she propped her head onto her hand, as he had done. "Is there a problem with that? I leave on that trip next Monday and won't see you for a couple of weeks."

"A week ago, I thought you hated me, and now you're inviting me to stay overnight?"

"*Hate* is a strong word. I was torn between attraction and aggravation."

"And now?" he asked.

"You're probably still going to aggravate me at some point, but the attraction is very strong."

"I'll work hard not to aggravate you, because I feel that same attraction."

Wednesday morning, Shane walked out to Norah's kitchen, dressed in navy slacks, a white shirt, and a light-blue tie. He'd pulled his hair into a tidy bun.

Norah put her arms around him and ran her hands up and down his back. "Dressed-up you is really something. I'd pop the buttons off that shirt if we didn't both have obligations."

Shane buried his face in her hair and drank in her scent. The two nights he'd spent with her had been mind-blowing. Now he needed to get his head back to business.

He picked up the travel mug Norah had filled with coffee. "I'll see you Friday. Around five?"

"Actually..." She paused. "I've got a work thing at the Sidecar. I don't plan to stay long, but it'll probably be seven before I'm home."

Shane waited for her to ask him to join her, but she didn't. "You won't drink and drive, will you?"

"No, I promise. One drink with my colleagues, and then I'll head home. You're sweet to worry."

Chapter Nineteen

Longing and Letting Go

Norah

NORAH WATCHED HER COLLEAGUES blowing off steam at the end of the week. The atmosphere was raucous, with lots of joking going on. She'd almost finished her drink, and she wouldn't have another. Ava and Wyatt couldn't keep their hands off each other, and Norah felt a pang of loneliness. It would be nice to have someone with her. Not someone—Shane. She knew he'd wanted her to ask him to join her, but she hadn't been able to get the words out.

How would I have introduced him? As my plumber? Do I want to admit I'm dating a plumber? Ava would have recognized him.

She could hear Caitlin screaming at her for being so elitest. *Are we even dating? I mean, really, we're just fuck buddies.*

She hated that term and shook her head, trying to clear it away. *Maybe friends with benefits is better. But are we friends?*

Monday night had been sex and more sex, but on Tuesday, they'd had a lengthy conversation about books they liked and about environmental concerns. He shared the devastation he'd seen near his home in California and how he'd moved to Vermont after a wildfire. He'd been evasive when she asked why he selected Vermont, but other than that, she'd enjoyed talking to him.

She looked at Ava and Wyatt again, their affection stirring her desire. Shane played her body like a maestro. Norah chuckled to herself, knowing how corny that sounded but not knowing how else to describe what he did to her. She'd orgasmed every time they came together, and that had never happened with Tom or even every time with Sam. She couldn't wait to get home to him. Her enthusiasm for the trip with Betsy had waned a bit.

What is wrong with me? I've guarded against letting a man become that central to my life since I started dating, and why would I want to change now? Especially for someone I only met a couple of months ago and have been intimate with for less than two weeks.

She drained her glass and stood, tapping Ava on the shoulder. "I'm going to head home. There's a lot to do before I leave on Monday. I'll see you in a couple of weeks."

Once in her car, she checked herself out in the mirror before turning the key in the ignition. *Thank goodness—I'm steady on my feet and I have the tiniest of tiny buzzes going on.*

She didn't want to break her promise to Shane. That thought stirred more confusion. One of her major life rules was not allowing a man to tell her how to act, yet she'd listened when Shane had told her not to drink and drive.

No, that wasn't listening to him. I wouldn't have had more than one, even without his warning. That's me being responsible.

Norah arrived home, and Shane and Gibbs walked to her car as she climbed out. Gibbs shook at her feet, waiting for her to pet him. She reached down and scratched his head, grateful for the diversion. She was a mass of emotions—shy about seeing Shane after the intimacy they'd shared but twitching with desire. The throbbing between her legs started the second she saw him, and she was already wet enough for him to take her right here on the lawn.

"Hi. Have you been here long?" Her fingers itched to stroke the muscles clearly visible under his gray T-shirt.

"Twenty minutes or so." Shane studied her. She was wearing tight jeans that clung to her hips and a purple tank top that revealed a hint of cleavage. Her denim jacket shielded his view, and her hair was pulled into a high ponytail. He leaned down and kissed the back of her neck, moving the ponytail out of his way. "Gibbs has been looking for Piper."

"Sorry, Gibbs." Norah petted his head again. "You're stuck with just me this weekend."

"Just you is fine." Shane put his arm over her shoulder and pulled her close. "More than fine. I like this look."

"We go casual on Fridays in the summer." She could barely get the words out. Looking up at him, she demanded, "Kiss me."

Shane's mouth crashed into hers as his arms wrapped around her. Norah moved her hands up his back and tangled her fingers in his hair, which he'd left down. Her lips moved under his, and a soft sigh escaped her. His hands moved to her hips, and she could feel his erection through his jeans.

He eased his hold and broke off the kiss to murmur, "I was going to take it slow tonight."

"No." Norah moved her lips back to his and slipped her hand between them, bringing her fingers to his bulge.

Dropping his arms, Shane grinned. "Let's go."

They hurried to the house. Norah fumbled in her purse, looking for her house key. Shane grabbed the purse and dumped it out on the table.

He plucked a key from the pile. "This one?" When she nodded, he worked the lock, opened the door, and stepped back, allowing her to enter first. He shoved the door shut with a bang and pointed at the kitchen, looking at Gibbs. "Stay."

He turned to face Norah. She yanked his shirt over his head and lowered her mouth to take one of his nipples between her teeth. She felt him shudder and heard his low moan as she alternated between gentle bites and swirling her tongue over the nub. His hands moved to his jeans, and Norah heard the zipper being lowered. Raising her head, she watched him shove the jeans to the ground and step over them. Her breath caught at the sight of his erection. Even after the three nights they'd spent together, its size still surprised her.

His eyes were dark with desire as he removed first her jacket then her tank top and, in one motion, unhooked her bra. As he dropped it to the floor, his mouth encircled a breast, and he sucked hungrily. His hands roamed over her body, and everywhere he touched felt like it was ablaze. She tried and failed to unzip her jeans without losing the contact between Shane's mouth and her breast. His hands moved to her jeans, but he was unsuccessful as well. Separating from her, he fondled her hips and her butt before moving back to the zipper and finally sliding it down. Shane bent to help her step out of them, and when he saw her black thong, he dropped to his knees. He grabbed the thong with his teeth, eased it over her legs, then sat on the floor, looking up at her.

Norah met his gaze, wondering what he was going to do next. She considered moving closer, but before she could, he stood, picked her up, and lowered her onto his cock, taking her breath away. She was at the perfect height for his mouth to reach her breasts. His tongue teasing the nubs and his cock thrusting into her brought her to the edge.

"Hold on." Shane had barely spit the words out before he exploded into her.

After catching his breath, he shifted her off his cock and cradled her in his arms. His fingers played with her clit, bringing her back to the edge and beyond. He sank to the floor and leaned against the wall, still holding her. As his breath returned to normal, he nuzzled her neck then reached up to pull the elastic off her ponytail. He sighed as he buried his face in her hair.

Several minutes passed, with neither of them moving. Finally, Norah said, "I rarely sit naked in my entryway."

"That's a pity, because you have a beautiful body. Not that you haven't looked gorgeous every time I've seen you, but naked Norah is something special."

She felt her cheeks flush. "You're not bad yourself." She eased herself off his lap and stood, reaching her hand back to him. "We should get dressed or..."

Shane wrapped his arms around her, and Norah savored the feeling of her body against his.

"Or what?" he asked.

"I don't even know." She sighed. "It seems wrong to sit here naked."

"Oh, honey." He chuckled. "It's so right. But okay, let's put some clothes on." He reached for his jeans.

"You don't have to put your shirt on. I quite like looking at your chest."

"Can I make the same request?" He smirked, and his eyes held a challenge.

"No." She tittered and pulled her tank top over her head, leaving her bra on the floor. "But I'll give you this."

"Nice. I like that look." He reached out and cupped a breast then rubbed his thumb over the nipple, which hardened instantly.

"Stop!" She batted his hand away. "Didn't you get enough?"

"No." His smile radiated affection. "I'm not sure I'll ever get enough of you."

Norah rolled her eyes. "Are you hungry? I had nachos at the Sidecar, but I probably have something in the kitchen."

"I ate before I got here. But I'd love to share a glass of wine with you."

They settled on the love seat, and Shane put his arm over her shoulders, making sure she was tight against him.

"I have a question." Norah had wanted to ask it since Monday.

"What?"

"Are you in trouble? You mentioned seeing your lawyer."

Shane chuckled. "No. It was about a business matter."

"This or that, huh? Did it go well?"

"Yes, very well. Does this mean now I can ask you something?" he asked, and she nodded. "Will you tell me about Piper's father?"

"What do you want to know?" *Is that any of his business?* Shane had shared nothing about his dating past.

"My dating life is an open book," he said, as if reading her mind. "I've never been in a romantic relationship that lasted more than a year. I went through a wild phase that lasted into my late twenties, and I was with a lot of women." He looked at her with a sheepish grin. "Life knocked me down a peg—my father's words—when I was twenty-eight and recovering from that included becoming much more discerning about the women I let into my life. You had a child with someone, and you don't seem like the type of woman to do that lightly. It must have been a serious relationship."

"How old are you?"

He smiled indulgently. "I'm forty. But after my heartfelt confession about what a hound dog I was, I think it's your turn to answer my question."

"We met when I represented my agency on one of his projects. We dated, we had fun, and the sex was good." She looked at Shane with the same sheepish grin. "I like sex."

"I've noticed."

"Eight months later, I was pregnant," she said, and Shane raised his eyebrows. "I had to do a course of antibiotics, and they interfered with my birth control. A baby was the last thing I wanted at that point in my life." She took a sip of wine and twirled the glass. "I thought about terminating the pregnancy. That idea horrified Sam. We fought about it for a week until my first doctor's appointment. Sam insisted on hearing the heart-beat, and that was the end of the argument. I had this miracle growing inside me. I couldn't get rid of that." She took another swallow of wine and stared at the glass. "I don't tell many people that."

Shane put his hand on her cheek and turned her face toward him. "Thank you for trusting me with it. How long did you stay together?"

"Eight years. I moved out of our house almost two years ago. You need to understand—I love Piper with all my heart, but I question my ability as a mother every single day."

"Oh, honey, I've watched you with her. You're fine. She told me last weekend that you'd done her braids—that you'd been practicing. She was proud of that."

"I heard her talking to you that first day about how Sam does a better job with her hair. My competitive nature kicked in." She shrugged.

"Do you get along well?"

"We do now. He was furious with me when I left, but we've ironed things out. He wanted to be married and have more kids. And now he has that. Or hopefully, he will soon. He and Sophie are trying to have a baby. Sophie's amazing. I couldn't ask for a better person to share Pip with. I'm happy he's got what he wants."

"What about you? Do you have what you want?"

Chapter Twenty

Meeting Mitzi

Shane

"*STAY IS A CHARMING* word in a friend's vocabulary."

Marcia's morning quote swirled in Shane's mind while he took Gibbs outside. When he and the dog had walked back into Norah's bedroom, she'd crawled between the sheets.

"He sleeps on the bed with me," he said.

Norah's expression told him this would be a first.

"He'll stay down at the bottom." Shane peeled off his jeans and boxers. "And if you get frisky, he'll jump off."

"If *I* get frisky? I'm not the one climbing in here naked." She'd put on the yellow satin pajamas he'd seen that first night. "What are you expecting?"

"I'm not the one who admitted I like sex." He stretched his arm across the pillow, and she settled against him. He pulled the blanket up to their chins.

"You don't have to admit anything," she said. "Your actions speak louder than your words."

By morning, Gibbs had inched his way closer to Shane, and Norah's side of the bed was empty. Shane's habit of writing late into the night had wrecked his sleep pattern, and he had lain awake for a long time, holding Norah and listening to her even breathing. It wasn't surprising she'd woken up before him.

When he wandered into the kitchen, he found her sitting at the table, doing a crossword puzzle. Half a dozen doughnuts sat on a plate, and he could smell the freshly brewed coffee.

"There's a coffee shop in town with the best doughnuts. You didn't seem likely to wake up for a while, so I drove over to buy us breakfast."

"You've already been out and about? I feel like a slacker." He took a bite of a raspberry-filled jelly doughnut and let out a moan. "This is delicious."

"Best doughnuts for miles." She watched him demolish the sweet pastry and wash it down with black coffee. "It wasn't so bad sharing the bed with Gibbs."

Shane gave her his most brilliant smile. "It's even better in cold weather when you can warm your feet under him. I'm glad you enjoyed it."

"I enjoyed the entire night. But now I need to pack," Norah said.

Full of coffee and doughnuts, he threw himself into the plumbing project. Late that afternoon, Norah came to the basement and sat on the stairs, watching Shane finish up. "I know nothing about plumbing, but it looks better down here."

"Yeah, it's coming together. It won't take much longer."

"Why don't you do this full-time? You're obviously good at it."

"This is a straightforward job, relatively speaking. I've been in some situations that are horrendous. You haven't lived until you've worked in backed-up sewer water." He grinned at her. "I could probably find some to take you to if you'd like a visual."

"I'll pass, thanks."

"Wise choice. Because I don't depend on this, I can be picky about what jobs I take."

"Fitting them in around this and that?"

Shane smiled. "Yup." He took her hand. "Let's go find something more exciting than plumbing to occupy us."

The next morning, Shane pulled on his boxers and went in search of Norah. Gibbs was by his side, and he barked as they approached the kitchen then bounded through the doorway to an older woman standing in the exact spot where Shane and Norah had sat naked Friday night. The woman recoiled at Gibbs's approach, and her eyes opened wide at the sight of Shane.

Shane had lived in California society long enough to recognize her designer clothes and skillful facelift. He also knew she had to be Norah's mother. All conversation stopped when he entered the room.

Norah turned to face him, and he smiled then winked at her. He stepped toward the woman with his hand extended. "Hello. I'm Shane Hilliker. You must be Norah's mother—the resemblance is hard to miss. And now I know where she gets her beauty from."

Shane didn't miss the split second it took the woman to grasp his hand. Deciding to really horrify her, he said, "I'm redoing her plumbing."

After a long sigh, Norah finally found her voice. "Shane, you're correct. This is my mother, Mitzi Taylor."

"Pleased to meet you." He dropped her hand. "I'm going to get a cup of coffee, and I'll get out of your hair." He walked to the coffeepot, making sure Mitzi had a good view of his butt—clad in nothing but form-fitting jersey boxers—and the tattoo that adorned his back. "I'll be in the living room, hon, watching the weather."

Holy crap. And I thought Norah was a bitch. He turned the television on, purposely leaving the volume low, hoping he'd be able to hear Norah's conversation with her mother.

"*That's* your replacement for Tom?" The disdain dripped from Mitzi's mouth.

"He's not a replacement for anyone, Mother."

"He seems very comfortable in your little home." There was a long pause. "Really, Norah. A plumber? What are you thinking?"

"Don't you need to be on your way?"

Shane heard the door open, then one more sentence from Mitzi. "I didn't think it was possible, but you've sunk even lower than Sam."

The door closed. Gibbs put his head on Shane's knee. "I don't think she liked me, buddy."

When Norah didn't join him, he walked to the kitchen, where she was standing at the sink, gazing vacantly out the window. He put his hands on her shoulders and turned her to face him.

"I. Am. So. Sorry." She paused between each word. "She's insufferable."

"Do you think it was the tats? Or the hair? Or maybe it was the sight of my ass in boxers."

Norah rubbed her forehead and shook her head.

"Norah." He grasped her hand. "I learned a long time ago not to worry about people who form an opinion about me based on my appearance. But I'm sorry that apparently, your association with me is going to cause problems with your mother."

"It's not a big deal."

"Don't bullshit me." He put his fingers under her chin and lifted it so that she could look into his eyes. "I can tell this bothers you. Let me know what you need from me. We can end this right now. I'll finish your plumbing, and you'll never see me again."

"That's not what I want. I don't care what my mother thinks."

"Do not bullshit me. And more importantly, don't bullshit yourself." He took the elastic off his wrist and pulled his hair into a ponytail. "I need to put some clothes on and get to work."

Late that afternoon, Norah sat on the basement stairs, the same way she had the day before. Shane had finished his work for the day and stood in front of her. "I have another question." When Norah cocked her head, he asked, "Who's Tom?"

"He's a colleague I dated for a few months last year."

"He met your parents?"

"We went on a cruise the day after Christmas." She closed her eyes, expelling a long sigh. "On our way to the airport, we stopped for Christmas dinner with my family."

"Not just met the parents—shared Christmas dinner with them." Shane nodded as he spoke. For some reason, the idea of

Norah being serious enough about someone to introduce him to her family bothered him. And the idea of another man enjoying her body infuriated him. *I'm being completely irrational.*

"I ended it as soon as we came home from the cruise."

He wanted to ask why.

"Sit." She waved at the stair below her. When he'd settled, she took his hand and nestled a key into the palm then folded his fingers over it. "Don't go home tonight." Norah was leaving for the airport at five in the morning. Their plan was to say their goodbyes when he finished work that day. "That's my extra house key. I'll leave as I planned, but you can sleep as late as you like and lock up when you leave. And if you want to work on the job while I'm gone, you'll be able to get in." She took his hand holding the key in hers and looked into his eyes. "Please stay."

Three days later, the text messages started arriving. Every afternoon, his phone pinged, and he found pictures of tourist spots in Italy. The last picture was always of Norah smiling broadly. She'd been gone almost two weeks when photos taken in Venice arrived, accompanied by a text.

> *I'll be home tomorrow around five pm. Piper is going with Sam and Sophie to Rhode Island for Sophie's mother's birthday. It would be nice to have a welcoming committee. Perhaps a dog and a tattooed plumber.*

His heart skipped a beat. He was at Norah's house, finishing a surprise for her. He'd go home, work late into the night, and be back at the house when she arrived. The contract for *Beneath the Burning Sky* was still not complete, and he was rereading the book, knowing he'd need to do a thorough analysis. This would be his first time adapting an existing work into a screenplay, and writing a screenplay was a different process from writing a novel. He needed to rediscover those muscles. In the next few weeks, he'd also have to work on edits for *Love, Lies, and Lethal Secrets*. His chest hurt, and he took a deep breath, reminding himself to breathe. Time with Norah had displaced his usual mechanisms for guarding against being overwhelmed, and he needed to get back on track.

So, work tonight, the lake tomorrow, and be back here to meet her.

After a long paddle, Shane arrived at Norah's house well before five. He grabbed a ball, let Gibbs out of the truck, and started playing fetch with him. His heart was pounding, and he hoped playing with Gibbs would calm his excitement. The plan worked until Norah's car turned into the driveway, and the pounding started again. He watched her climb out of the car, hoping his grin didn't look too silly. Gibbs bounded to her, and stood at her feet, waiting to be petted.

"He's excited to see you!" Shane called across the space between them.

"Is he the only one?"

"Not at all." Shane loped across the drive and hugged her. Burying his face in her hair, he said, "You feel good. I've missed you."

"Don't sniff me. I feel like I've been up for days, and I'm sure I stink. I need a shower."

He soaked in the feel of her against him. "I have a surprise for you." Reluctantly, he let her go and removed her suitcase from the car. At the door, he used the key she'd given him.

"Have you spent any time here?" she asked.

"A little." He took her hand and led her through the house, out the back door, and onto the deck.

"What's that?" Norah was looking at the structure to the left of the deck, which hadn't been there when she'd left.

Shane grinned widely. "It's an outdoor shower. Come see."

They walked from the deck, following the steppingstones he'd placed the day before. He opened the door and let Norah go up the two steps ahead of him. The dressing area contained shelves—with fluffy white towels—a bench, and hooks. Hanging from one of the hooks was a white robe. A Boston fern hung in one corner, and Edison light bulbs were strung along the walls. Two steps led down to the shower. Built-in niches held shampoo, conditioner, and body wash.

"This is amazing!" She kissed him then looked around as if trying to absorb it all.

"The outdoor-shower season isn't very long here, but I thought you and Piper might enjoy it." He'd been nervous that building the shower might come across as presumptuous, but her reaction told him it hadn't. Her delight filled him with joy. "Do you want to try it out?"

"I do. It's exactly what I need." She peeled off her clothes. "Are you going to join me? It looks big enough for both of us."

"I was hoping you'd notice that." After a couple of minutes in the water, Shane asked, "Can I wash your hair?"

She nodded, and he worked the shampoo through, gently massaging her scalp, loving her soft sighs of pleasure. After moving her under the water to rinse out the bubbles, he picked up the shower gel and soaped her body. His erection longed for her touch, but he knew she needed to relax.

When all the soap was gone, he enveloped her in his arms. "Ready to get out?" At another nod, he let her climb back to the dressing area ahead of him. He handed her a towel and used another one to dry her hair.

She plucked the robe off the hook, slipped her arms into it, then handed him a dry towel, which he secured around his waist. "You need a robe."

"I didn't want to make assumptions. I love how private your backyard is. It's the perfect place for something like this." A heavy tree line formed her north and south property lines, and a gentle stream flowed along the western boundary.

"Yes, I enjoy having neighbors close by, but not so close that they can see everything I do." They stepped out of the dressing area and back onto the walking path Shane had created. "Although this is about the most scandalous thing I've ever done. I'm known for being straitlaced."

"Anyone who thinks you're straitlaced has never seen you in the bedroom."

Chapter Twenty-One

Shane's Not Invited

Norah

"I HATE TO TELL you this, but I'm exhausted." Norah had hoped the shower would wake her up, but she could barely keep her eyes open.

"It's okay. Mind if I lie with you?"

"Please do." She snuggled contentedly against Shane. It felt good to be in her own bed. "Have you ever been to Italy?" Her voice was sleepy.

"Yes, it's beautiful. I loved the pictures you sent, and I can't wait to hear all about the trip."

"Everywhere we went, all I could think of was how much I'd like to be there with you. To make love with you there..." Her voice trailed off as sleep overtook her.

Several hours later, she woke up. Shane had rolled away from her, and his steady breathing told her he was asleep. Gibbs lay at the foot of the bed, snoring softly.

An outdoor shower. I can't believe he built that for me. She reached up to feel her hair, knowing it must be a mess. She was hungry and needed to pee, but both of those were overridden by her desire for Shane.

Her words as she was falling asleep came back to her. *I told him I want to make love. We haven't used the L word. It's always been sex. We've been having sex.*

Norah eased her way off the bed and went to the bathroom. As she washed her hands, she shook her head at the vision in the mirror. *My hair is a rat's nest.* Deciding on food could wait. She eased back into bed and slid all the way over to Shane. Her body spooned against his, and her hand reached for his cock. It hardened quickly, and his breathing changed. When Shane rolled onto his back, Gibbs jumped off the bed.

"I told you he'd jump off if you got frisky." His voice was husky. His hands rubbed up and down her back, and he started to roll on top of her.

"No." Norah pushed him back to the mattress and climbed on top of him. Her lips went to his, hungry for his taste.

Shane lay mostly motionless. "Tell me what you want."

"Let me show you." She moved to his neck then continued nibbling her way down to his chest. Her tongue drew circles around his nipple, her touch as light as a feather. She could tell he was struggling not to move, and she took the nub between her teeth and nipped at it.

Shane groaned, and his hips shifted. Norah alternated circling with her tongue and nipping at him, relishing his failure to restrain himself. His hands moved to her butt and stroked with a pressure that increased every time her teeth grazed him. His fingers moved between her cheeks, and Norah drew in a sharp breath as her heartbeat increased.

"Two can play at your game." His finger moved, breaching her hole, and Norah became the one shifting her hips.

She continued working her way down his body, moving her ass out of his reach. Her kisses followed the line downward from his belly button, and when her mouth reached his cock, she enveloped him. He stayed still as she sucked his head and stroked the shaft.

Finally, he murmured, "I'm close."

Norah moved away from him. She wanted to feel him explode inside her. She'd pictured her orgasms with him in every bed she'd slept in while she was gone, and now she wanted all of him.

"Do that thing you do to my clit," she said, moving back up the bed to lie beside him.

"What thing? This thing?" His fingers played with her. He never had to struggle to find the right spot, and she never failed to respond.

"Yes, the thing that no other guy has ever done in quite the same way." She tried in vain to remain still until finally, she climbed on top and guided him in. "I missed this."

After drinking in the way he filled her, she started to move, and Shane matched her rhythm. Without even needing his fingers on her clit, she exploded, and as the waves washed over her, Shane continued to thrust until his orgasm hit.

Panting, Norah collapsed on top of him. "I missed you."

"Daddy!" Piper hopped out of Norah's car, raced across the yard, and flung herself into Sam's waiting arms.

Norah had taken her for a haircut after school, and Sam was talking to Shane while he waited for them to get home. *This should be interesting.*

Three weeks had passed since she returned from Italy, and Shane had become a regular visitor. He never stayed when Piper was with her, though he and Gibbs had come for dinner more than once when she was there, and they'd all gone to the lake. But Sam had not met Shane and, unless Piper had said something, didn't even know Norah was seeing him.

Piper scrambled out of Sam's arms and threw herself down to hug Gibbs. Looking up from the ground, she said, "Hi, Shane."

"Hi, Pip. I like your haircut." Shane chuckled as Norah walked over to them. "I'm last in the pecking order." He looked at Sam. "As I should be." His glance shifted back to Norah. "Do you want me to get Piper's bag?"

"That would be great." She handed him her keys, feeling foolish because he still had the key she'd given him before she left, but she wasn't sure she wanted Sam to know about it.

"I thought the plumbing job was finished." Sam smirked at her.

"It is."

"He seems like a nice guy. And Piper clearly loves the dog. All we hear is Gibbs this and Gibbs that."

"Me too."

"Piper says he built you an outside shower," Sam said, and Norah nodded. "You'll have to drain that when it gets colder. Sorry for telling you what to do. Wanted to be sure you know."

"I do. He told me."

They said their goodbyes. As Sam drove away with Piper, Shane said, "He seems like a nice guy."

"He said the same thing about you." She chuckled.

"We had an interesting discussion about the benefits of pets."

The chuckle turned into a groan.

"I think it's interesting that he won't get a pet unless you do, because he doesn't want to be ahead of you in the parenting sweepstakes. His words," Shane continued.

"We've talked often about how parenting Piper is not a competition."

"Not every guy would be that sensitive. Can I ask another question?"

Norah nodded. She liked the way he always sought her permission before asking something that might be awkward.

"Will you tell me what happened between you?"

They had made their way into the house while they were talking, and Norah stopped in the kitchen. "Let's have some wine."

She poured two glasses and led him to the love seat. *How much do I want to tell him?*

"When Piper was about four and a half, she developed a stutter. We tried counseling, but nothing helped, and eventually, we realized it was the tension between Sam and me that caused it." She took a sip of the wine while Shane looked at her expectantly. "Sam would tell you that his messiness, scattered nature, and constant tardiness caused the tension."

"What would Norah tell me?" Shane squeezed her hand.

"Norah would tell you she had her tubes tied and didn't tell him." She looked at Shane. "I'm a terrible person, right?"

"You must have had your reasons."

"Sam wanted more kids. He started making noise about it when Piper was almost three. I was afraid he'd be able to talk me into it, and that was the last thing I wanted." She described the business trip when she'd had it done and how bitchy she'd been to Sam when she returned. "I didn't regret my decision, but it was a huge thing to have between us, and the relationship deteriorated from there." She drained her wine glass. "I've righted most of the wrongs I did to him, but Sam still doesn't know."

"I knew you didn't want more children, but I didn't know your feelings were that strong."

"I feel like I have more to offer the world than raising children. It all goes back to my mother." She went to the kitchen to refill their wineglasses, talking as she poured. "I know that's such a cliché, but I figured it out when we were in counseling." She rejoined him. "My mother is brilliant. She majored in biology in college and was ready to go to grad school for a degree in microbiology so she could go into medical research. Her senior year, she met my father. He was older and already established in his career. They got married right after she graduated, and one week into her first semester of grad school, he got a job opportunity in Paris. She withdrew from school, and they moved to France. They were there for seven years and had my sister, Judith. They were expecting me when they finally came back here. My father works in international finance, and there's a lot of socializing that goes along with that. My mother became his hostess and a mother to my siblings and me. I feel like she could have done more important things with her life. I grew up determined not to follow in her footsteps."

"I gather from her reaction to me that she has higher expectations for you than a plumber."

"Yes. They had high expectations for my siblings and me. We all went to Ivy League universities, but that wasn't enough. We each needed to choose the right partner. Someone who was our equal. They tolerated Sam because he was Pip's father, but once he was out of the picture, she began mentioning eligible men, and my father increased the pressure for me to leave Vermont—to go somewhere that I could get a bigger, more important job and meet a more appropriate man."

"Any plans to do that?"

"Not in the immediate future. Or even in the long term. Sam and I co-parent well. I will not upset that." She stood and reached for his glass. "More wine?" When she came back with full glasses, she asked, "What about you? Did you ever want kids?"

"I didn't grow up pining to be a father. If I'd stayed with a woman for more than a year and she wanted children, I wouldn't have objected. I have a niece and nephew, both teenagers now, and I have friends with kids whom I love. But I don't feel a big lack in my life because I'm not a father."

What a refreshing attitude.

On Monday, Norah said, "I'm going to have Pip tomorrow night." They'd just gone to bed.

"In other words, make myself scarce."

Norah nodded sheepishly.

"Why the change? I thought you and Sam tried to keep the schedule consistent," Shane said.

"We do. I'm going to Connecticut on Thursday. There's a big party for my father's seventieth birthday on Friday night. I've been commanded to get there early to help."

"Piper's not going?"

"There was a family party in the summer. This one is formal. Black tie, and no kids are invited."

"Oh."

More than two hundred people filled the country club in Greenwich, and Norah realized she knew only a handful of them. White lights twinkled throughout the ballroom and a string quartet provided background music. The black silk of Norah's off-the-shoulder dress clung to her body down to her hips, where it erupted with cascading ruffles that reached the floor, giving it a playful look. Her mother had insisted that Norah and her sisters wear black, and her father had presented them with diamond necklaces.

Betsy looped her arm around Norah. "Mom and Dad are in their glory." Dinner had been served, toasts had been made, and the rest of the evening would be dedicated to dancing and socializing.

"How soon do you think I can go?" Norah asked.

"Don't leave me here alone."

"You're not alone. You have the perfect Percy with you."

"He's not perfect," Betsy protested.

But Norah knew from the sparkle in her sister's eyes that she had no complaints about her boyfriend of one year. He'd opened an outdoor adventure center in Colorado six months earlier, which had become an instant success. *And of course, that success endeared him to Mommy and Daddy dearest.*

When Betsy left her to dance with Percy, Norah took a deep breath and started moving around the ballroom, speaking with people she'd known as a child. She employed all her charm-school skills and hated every minute of it. A tap on her shoulder startled her, and she turned to find herself face-to-face with a classmate from high school.

"I've been trying to catch up with you all night." The handsome, clean-cut man reached out to hug her. "You look good, Norah."

"Artemis Winters. I don't think I've seen you since graduation, Artie. Weren't you in London?"

"London, Tokyo, Berlin. I've been in New York since the beginning of the year."

"International banking?" When he nodded, she added, "My mother keeps me up-to-date."

"As does mine. You're saving the environment in Vermont?"

"Yes. Are you here with your parents? I should say hello to them."

"No, I'm here solo. Your mother invited me. She said you're single and that with some attention from the right man, perhaps you'd be ready to come back to the city."

Norah froze. *My God. She's setting me up.* She wanted to scream, but charm and grace bubbled over her anger. This wasn't Artie's fault. She remembered him fondly. "My mother misrepresented my status. Did she tell you I have an eight-year-old daughter?"

Artie's eyes widened. "She did not."

"I share custody with her father and have no plans to upset that arrangement. And... I like my life in Vermont." She managed to grin. "I'm sorry you got caught up in my mother's machinations."

"I know how parents can be. Mine are disappointed I'm not married and the father of a couple of kids." He kissed Norah's cheek. "I'm going to head out. It was good to see you, even under false pretenses."

Norah ended her facade of being interested in any of the guests. She pictured Shane on her arm, with his long hair flowing. She'd proudly introduce him as her plumber, describing how he saved her house.

I should have invited him. I know he wanted me to. She shook her head, growing angrier, not only at her mother but at herself. *I'm done with this. Cait is right, I need to stop trying to please my parents. My life is good. I'm doing important work. I have an extraordinary child.* She remembered how she'd told Artemis she liked her life in Vermont. *It's true. And I want more with Shane. I've told him all the bad parts about me, and he hasn't run away. He's respectful and kind. I wish he was here. He'd love this dress.*

Norah was disappointed to find her driveway empty the next day. She had fantasized the entire way home and couldn't wait to feel Shane's hands on her.

The house was unnaturally quiet when she walked in, and a sense of unease overtook her. In the kitchen, she found a note anchored by the key she'd given him weeks earlier.

My Dearest Norah,

I've discovered that I was less than truthful when I told you I didn't care if people judged me on my appearance, because I've found it matters very much to me that I was not good enough to attend your father's birthday party. I lay there expectantly Monday night, holding you in my arms, waiting for you to ask me to accompany you. Your silence spoke volumes.

You may be surprised to learn that I own a tuxedo and know how to comport myself in high society. And believe it or not, I can make conversation far beyond pipe fittings and water heaters.

As much as I love being with you, and I love it very much, if I'm not <u>good</u> enough to be with you in public, then I do not <u>want</u> to be with you in private.

My father will be here in three weeks, and we will install the heat pump because, as I told you, I honor my commitments. I'll be in touch to arrange access. Otherwise, I won't bother you again.

Shane

Chapter Twenty-Two

Writer's Block

Shane

SHANE CRUMPLED THE PAPER into a ball and tossed it toward the wastebasket in the corner. It fell short and joined the others littering the floor. He hadn't written with pen and paper in years, but after days of sitting at his keyboard with no words coming, he had to try something different.

And that's not working any better. Nor did changing my location.

He'd moved from the desk to the couch in his study and discovered that, as good as the couch was for late-afternoon naps, it was worthless for pulling words out of his ass. So were the counter in his kitchen, his bed, and even a local coffee shop. He stretched his arms over his head and looked toward Gibbs, who slept peacefully on the couch.

I'm glad he can sleep, because just as words aren't coming, neither is sleep.

Two weeks had passed since he'd written the note and left Norah's key on the counter. Two weeks and three days since he'd seen her—since they'd made love that moved from raging passion to tender sweetness in the blink of an eye and since he'd held her, waiting for an invitation that never came. They parted on Tuesday morning, with Norah telling him she'd be back on Saturday. On Friday, he returned to her house, gathered his belongings that had accumulated there, and wrote the note.

On Saturday, a text arrived from Norah.

I'm at the Welcome Center in Brattleboro. Just a little over an hour until I'm home. I can't wait to see you. Well, actually, I want to do a lot more than just see you. I'm sorry I didn't ask you to come with me. I have a lot I want to tell you.

Shane had blocked her number immediately. It didn't matter what she had to say to him. He'd known he would miss her, but he hadn't realized how deep into his soul her absence would travel.

"Gibbs! Let's go for a walk."

Shane's property covered forty acres, and he was sure he'd traversed every one of them in the past two weeks. *Anything to avoid my laptop.* He snorted as they reached the pinnacle of his land. One of the first things he'd done three years ago was place a chair in the clearing.

He sank into it. Gibbs flopped at his feet, and Shane scratched the dog's head. "You don't know what you're missing, not looking at this view."

The chair faced east, and the Connecticut River, which ran between Vermont and New Hampshire, was visible in the distance. Even farther away were the White Mountains. A brilliant blue sky showed off Vermont's renowned fall colors, slightly shy of their peak.

Mom and Dad picked exactly the right week to come. And I have got to get some writing done before they arrive.

The contract for *Beneath the Burning Sky* had been signed a month earlier, and Shane had completed the preliminary work. He'd identified the most important story elements and developed the three-act structure. He'd had to eliminate four characters and their subplot, but he was sure at least two of them would return in the next movie—because he was positive there would be more.

Yeah, if I can get this first one written. Some events in the story had to be shifted, and Shane had developed an extensive outline so he didn't miss anything. That had all been done before Norah went to Connecticut for the big party, and he'd thought writing the screenplay would be a breeze.

Instead, he was spending his time trying to figure out if he'd made the right decision in walking away from Norah. *Should I have been more forthcoming about my writing?* The last thing he wanted was acceptance or desire because of his fame. He'd had that life in California and found it hollow and meaningless. His relationships there lived and died on what people thought he could do for them. Norah wasn't like that. He was sure of it. But—and this was a big but—she obviously wanted someone who fit in with her high-society family.

I don't want to be accepted just because I'm a best-selling author.

Yet the fact that he'd been less than honest with her ate at him. Especially in light of her confession that she'd had her tubes tied without telling Sam. *I hid a major part of me because I didn't want her to be drawn to me because of it. And she did exactly the opposite—told me her deepest secret, knowing it could make me view her unfavorably. She took a real risk, and I did not.*

He shifted his thoughts back to the screenplay. One thing making it so difficult to write was the environmental factor, because every word led him back to Norah and her passion about climate change. She could have been the main character in the movie—except, his main character was male. He had thought about changing *him* to *her* and had even run the idea by Marcia, who'd taken it to the producers. And the answer was exactly what he'd expected. The readers of the series were in love with Professor Dai Accosta and making him female would sink not just this movie but any future ones as well.

Shane leaned his head back against the chair and closed his eyes. *What about Isolde?* She was a minor female character. She was part of Dai's team but didn't have a backstory and wasn't significant. *But she could be. I'm going to build her story. The moviegoers can love Dai, but they're going to want to be Isolde. And Norah is going to be my muse. Isolde will pay homage to Norah.*

For the first time in two weeks, Shane was excited about the project. He nudged Gibbs with his toe. "Let's go, buddy. I've got writing to do."

Shane sat in the kitchen, holding his phone. His mother insisted on cooking, and he was keeping her company while his father napped in the living room. They'd arrived the day before, and today he had taken them hiking on his favorite trail. Then they'd spent the rest of the day driving around so his parents could get a good taste of the fall colors.

He visited absently with her and stared at Norah's number. He'd blocked it when he left her house, not wanting to hear from her. Rubbing his finger over her name, he stood.

"I'll be right back, Mom," he said, walking outside. "I need to make a call."

"Hello." Norah's voice was achingly familiar.

"Hey, it's Shane."

"Yes." Her tone was the same one she'd used with him when they first met, which wasn't a surprise.

"My parents are here. We spent today playing tourist, and if it works for you, I thought we could start on the heat pump tomorrow."

There was a long pause. "I'll leave the bulkhead unlocked so you can get into the basement. How late will you be here?"

"If you don't want to see me, we can be gone before you come home from work."

"Actually..." There was another long pause. "Will you bring Gibbs? Piper would love to see him."

"I'll bring him. And we'll stay until you get home."

Shane and his father were in the basement when he heard Piper outside.

"Gibbs! I've missed you."

He could tell they were rolling on the ground. He looked at his dad. "Wait till you see this little girl. She's something."

They stood at the top of the stairs, watching, until Piper noticed them.

"Shane!" She pulled herself away from the dog and launched herself into his arms, just as he'd watched her do with Norah and Sam.

He held onto her for a brief moment then placed her on the ground. "Pip, this is my dad. Dad, this is Piper Carpenter. She and Gibbs became good buddies while I was working here."

"I'm sad you don't come over anymore. I still don't have a dog." She pulled a pouty face and went back to playing with Gibbs.

"That was quite a greeting for a plumber," his father said.

"I hung out with her and her mother for a while."

"Another failed relationship?"

Shane shook his head. This was a recurring thread from his father. "Not sure it ever reached the level of a relationship."

"Your mother worries about you being alone."

"I'm fine, Dad."

They saw little of Norah until they were nearly finished on Saturday. His father was working in the basement while Shane worked on the unit in the living room. She watched him for a few minutes.

"Will you be finished today?" she asked.

Shane nodded. "Should be."

"I'm sorry I didn't ask you to go to my father's party."

Shane concentrated on the bolt he was working on. "Water over the dam."

He turned to face her, and the sight of her knocked away all rational thought. Her eyes held a multitude of emotions but none of the distrust he'd seen in the first few weeks he'd known her. He had a thousand things he wanted to tell her, and he didn't say any of them.

His father came upstairs at that moment. "I think we're done. Let's go over the things you need to know." He led her through the installation and pointed out the features one by one. At the end, he said, "If you have any problems, call Shane. He'll know how to fix them. It was nice meeting you. You picked out a good unit." He looked at Shane. "We should get out of here and let Norah have some peace." Shane didn't move. His father gave him a penetrating look. "Is there anything else?"

There wasn't, but Shane was having a hard time forcing his legs to walk out the door.

In the driveway, Piper hugged him. "Will you come back? Please?"

Shane held tightly to her for a few seconds. "That might be hard. I've got some projects keeping me busy. But Gibbs and I will always remember you. You're going to be a great dog mom someday."

Beneath the Burning Sky

Act II Opening Scene

FADE IN:

EXT. A PARK, EARLY EVENING

The park overlooking a river is deserted. Crops are growing on the other side of the river. Large-scale farm equipment litters the landscape.

PROFESSOR DAI ACCOSTA (43), unkempt college professor. His hair is shaggy, and his beard needs a trim. He stands on the bluff at the edge of the park, gazing at the other side with hollow eyes.

ISOLDE MONTAGUE (25) approaches from behind and taps Dai on the shoulder. Startled, the professor turned to face her.

DAI

How'd you find me?

ISOLDE

It wasn't hard. You've been here every day since the accident. Professor, I have something you need to hear.

She pulls out her phone and taps the play button.

The recording features two men.

"Do you think Accosta suspects us?" one voice says.

"No, the tampering was perfect. The police ruled it operator error," the second voice says.

"It did the job. Losing his wife and sons in that accident distracted him from his crusade against us. And now we have our permits, so there's nothing he can do."

ISOLDE stops the recording.

DAI

How did you get that? Who's speaking?

ISOLDE

Is that important? They admitted that Terra Global is responsible for the accident. Professor, they killed your wife and your sons! To distract you!

DAI brushes tears from his eyes and puts his hand over his mouth.

I don't know what to say.

ISOLDE grabs his arm. Professor... Dai, say you're going to fight. We're all with you. Terra Global is raping the earth. Think about the future. Think about your daughter. She's still here, but what kind of world will she inherit?

FADE OUT.

Shane pushed back from his desk, satisfied with his progress. Since his parents had left ten days before, he'd finished the first act and the opening for the second act. It was only midnight, but he was tired and ready to sleep. A month had passed since he'd written the note, and he was coping better than he had in the first two weeks. He missed Norah more than the other women he'd had brief interludes with, but that would fade with time. His father's words about "another failed relationship" still rankled.

Climbing between the sheets, he looked at Gibbs. "I guess you're going to be my only longtime companion."

Two hours later, he awoke to the sound of thunder in the distance. Gibbs, who didn't normally react strongly to weather, was uneasy. He jumped down and paced to the door and back then rested his nose on the bed and whined.

The storm must be strong for him to be this antsy. Shane reached his hand out to scratch the dog's head. "You're okay, buddy."

Seconds later, Shane's pager startled him: *Need you at the station. Flooding south of here.*

He jumped out of bed. *Damn, that must be what Gibbs is hearing.*

Soon after moving to Vermont, he'd joined the volunteer fire department, and six months later, they'd invited him to become a member of the Swift Water Rescue Team. They'd traveled up and down the East Coast, assisting during and after hurricanes and tropical storms. He threw his clothes on and ran outside. All his gear was in his truck, ready to respond whenever the call came.

Chapter Twenty-Three

Swift Water Rescue

Norah

"MOMMY." THE LIGHTNING FLASH illuminated Piper standing in the doorway to Norah's bedroom. "Can I get in bed with you? I'm scared." The crash of thunder obscured her words, but Norah knew she must be afraid.

"Come on in, baby girl." Norah reached over to turn on the bedside lamp and, when nothing happened, realized the power must be off.

She held Piper as the lightning flashed again, followed by an immediate clap of thunder. *This is right on top of us.* It felt like she'd been listening to the storm for hours. She'd never heard rain pounding on the roof as relentlessly as it was now.

This is when I don't enjoy living alone. I wish there were another adult here, because I'm hiding it from Pip, but I'm as scared as she is.

They clung to each other, jumping every time the room lit up with a lightning strike and at every thunderclap. Piper was crying gently. "I wish Daddy were here."

Me too. Norah lifted her phone off the charger. *I'll call him. Maybe that will make Pip feel better. He and Sophie must be getting the same...*

Before she could find his name, the noise outside increased. In addition to the rain and the constant rumble of thunder, it sounded like rocks were hitting the house.

"Mommy, what is that?" Piper asked through her tears.

"I don't know, but I think we should leave. Let me put some clothes on, and then I'll help you." She fumbled in the dark, looking for jeans and a sweatshirt.

"Leave?" Piper's voice held a hysterical tone. "Where will we go? It's pouring out. We'll get wet."

"We'll be okay." Norah shoved her feet into sneakers. "We'll go to Daddy's or Ava's." *God, I hope the water isn't over the road.* She turned on the flashlight on her phone. "Come on. Let's get you into some warm clothes." They made their way to the door.

"Wait! I want to take my unicorn!" Piper cried. The purple unicorn was her favorite stuffed animal.

"No, honey, we'll be back here in the morning. He'll be fine."

Norah was nervous. She knew the rocks must be coming from the stream on the back side of the house, but she didn't know how. The stream bed was several feet below her land. They'd had hard rainstorms before, but it had never flooded.

"Please, Mommy." Piper's crying intensified.

Norah took a deep breath. "Stay here. I'll get it." She ran to Piper's bedroom, grabbed the unicorn, raced back, and handed it to Pip. "Hold on tight."

She opened the door, and they stepped outside and into a disaster. Water swirled on both sides of her house, and as Norah turned the flashlight toward her car, she could see that the water was almost to the tops of the tires. Her heart pounded as she looked toward the road. They could walk to the road, but what then? The water was creeping closer to the porch, and she could hear rocks crashing against it.

We can't stay here. She called 911. "My daughter and I are at 106 Rock Maple Road. My house is nearly surrounded by water."

The operator told her that rescue personnel would be dispatched and said they should stay put. But Norah could see how much the water had risen in the few minutes they'd been on the porch, and she knew they needed to leave.

Grasping Piper's hand, she said, "We're going to walk up to the knoll. Do not let go of my hand."

Two steps led from the porch to the ground, and the water was lapping against the top one. She and Piper splashed down to the ground then walked up the hill, stepping out of the rising water, all the while being pelted with rain. Piper screamed at each bolt of lightning and clung to Norah's hand like a vise grip.

When they reached high ground, Norah looked around, realizing they had no path out. *Someone is going to have to come in a boat.* She had seen a video of rescues like that but didn't dream she would ever be part of one. She could feel Piper shivering at her side.

"I'm going to call Daddy." *He can't do anything for us, but Pip will feel better if she talks to him.*

Sam answered on the second ring, sounding sleepy. "Hey. What's up? Is something wrong?"

"Aren't you getting this storm?" Norah couldn't suppress the note of hysteria in her voice.

"It's raining, but nothing unusual. What's that noise?"

"It's rocks from the stream. My house is surrounded by water. We're standing on that little hill at the end of the driveway. I've called 911, but I don't know how we're going to get out of here, Sam." A sob tore out of her. *I can't cry. I need to be strong for Piper.*

"Oh my God. I'll be right there."

"No. You can't drive here. But talk to Pip. She's scared." Norah held the phone to her daughter's ear.

Piper's crying eased slightly as Sam talked to her. A deep roar sounded, and Norah turned to see her house ripped from its foundation.

"Holy shit! Sam, my house is gone! The water knocked it off the foundation, and it's floating away." She was crying now, nearly as hard as Piper.

"Norah, I'm going to the fire station to see if there's anything I can do. Climb to higher ground if you can."

Norah took several deep breaths and stopped crying. They were as high as they could go. She prayed silently that someone would come soon.

Piper saw the searchlights first. "Mommy, look."

Norah watched as the lights in the distance came closer and illuminated them, wet and shivering. The thunder and lightning had finally stopped, and the rain had diminished to a gentle shower. A voice called, "Hold on. We'll be there in no time."

My God, that sounds like Shane. She shook her head, sure that she was wrong.

But Piper recognized his voice too. "Mommy, that's Shane. He's going to save us."

The inflatable raft anchored close to the hill they were on. "Norah, Pip, it's Shane! We can't get any closer, but we're going to get you out of there. I need you to listen. Okay?"

"Tell us what to do," Norah said.

"I'm going to throw you a rope. It's got two life jackets on it. I need you to put one on yourself and then put one on Piper. Ready? Here it comes."

Norah missed it on the first throw. "Pip, I need to let go of your hand."

"No, Mommy. You said not to."

"I know, but I need to catch the rope that Shane is throwing to us. It'll just be for a minute."

Across the distance, Shane called, "You'll be okay, Piper. Your mom will catch the rope, and then she'll take your hand again."

Norah caught it on the next toss, and with shaking fingers, she freed the life preservers and put one on herself and the other on Piper. Norah's breath was uneven, and she was freezing. *I must keep it together, but how the hell are we going to get into that raft?*

"All right! I'm happy to see you with those on." Shane's voice was calm and reassuring. "Now, I'm going to throw another rope over. Pip, your mom is going to put that rope around you, and then you're going to jump into our raft."

"Jump? I can't do that."

"Yes, you can. I'm right here, and I'm going to catch you."

"Is Mommy going to jump?"

"After you," Norah said.

"Can't we jump together?"

"No. We need to get you and then your mom. You can do it," Shane said.

"What if I miss? I'll drown."

"No, you won't. You have the life vest on. Remember when we kayaked, and we talked about how those keep you safe? And if you land in the water, we'll pull you into the raft, using the rope. You can do this."

Norah listened to their exchange, every fiber of her being not wanting to let Piper jump but knowing there was no other way. She knelt and clutched Piper's shoulders. "Shane's right. You can do this. He's right there, waiting. He won't let anything happen to you." She stood up. "Be brave."

"We'll count to three and then you'll jump," Shane said. "Count with me. One, two, three."

Piper sailed through the air and into his arms. "I did it! I did it, Mommy!"

Sobs overtook Norah. *Piper is safe. She's okay.* "Yes, you did. I'm so proud of you, baby girl."

"Now you, Norah," Shane said, sounding relieved. "Catch the rope, put it under your arms, and we'll count it down. I might not catch you, hon, but there's a space on the raft waiting for you."

Norah missed the rope on the first and second toss. She could hear Piper telling her she could do it, but her hands were numb, and her whole body was trembling.

"Take a deep breath. I won't throw again until you're ready." There was no hint of a rush in Shane's voice.

She closed her eyes and took several deep breaths. *He called me hon.* She'd discouraged every man she'd ever been with from using terms of endearment. Shane hadn't done it often, but whenever he called her *honey* or *hon*, it warmed a piece of her heart.

She opened her eyes. "I'm ready. Try again." She grabbed the rope out of the air and placed it under her arms quickly, as Shane had instructed her.

"We'll count it down together, like I did with Piper. There's nothing to be afraid of. If you miss the boat, we'll have you out of the water in seconds. Let's go. One, two, three."

Norah didn't remember jumping. She remembered only landing with a thud, then arms were around her, followed by blankets—blessedly warm blankets. She lay on the bottom of the raft, with her head in Shane's lap and Piper lying on top of her.

"Let's get them back to the barn," a voice said.

The motor revved, and they sliced through the water. They reached several trucks, and someone lifted Pip off Norah and out of the raft.

"Put her in my truck. I'll drive them back to the station. The EMTs and Piper's father are there." Shane lifted Norah into the passenger side of his truck. Piper was in the middle, and he buckled them in then tucked dry blankets around them.

Sam and Sophie were waiting in the parking lot when Shane reached the station. He slid Piper out the driver's-side door and placed her in Sam's waiting arms.

"Daddy, our house is gone." She buried her face in Sam's shoulder. "I was so scared."

"When you're ready, have the EMTs check her out." Shane walked to the passenger side and lifted Norah out.

He placed her feet on the ground, and her knees buckled. He scooped her up and carried her to the waiting paramedics. After checking her over, they declared her free to go.

Norah was warming up. "Free to go where?"

They also checked Piper and released her. Sam had her back in his arms when he and Sophie approached Norah. "You have a place with us for as long as you need it."

Shane spoke up. "She's coming home with me."

Chapter Twenty-Four

Shelter From the Storm

Norah

NORAH HAD NEVER BEEN to his house and didn't even know exactly where he lived. For what felt like forever, they were in the truck. She didn't say a word. They'd given her scrubs at the firehouse, and the truck was warm, but she couldn't stop shaking. The sun was rising when Shane turned off the paved road and onto a narrow gravel road. Eventually, the tree-lined path opened to a meadow with a modern two-story home resting in the middle. She didn't move when they stopped. Shane scrambled out of the truck and over to the passenger door then reached to unbuckle her seat belt. After placing the blanket over her shoulders, he helped her out and led her inside.

The house was striking, with clean lines, tall windows, and hard wood floors, but Norah didn't notice any of that. She looked around blankly, overwhelmed by everything that had happened since Piper appeared in her doorway.

Turning to Shane, she said, "You saved us."

Her face crumpled, and he pulled her close, not saying anything, just holding her while she cried.

"Let's sit." He settled her on the leather couch in his living room, tossed aside the rough blanket from the firehouse, and replaced it with a cashmere one he kept close by for chilly nights. "I'll be right back." At the bar in the corner, he poured two shots of bourbon. He handed one to her and watched as she knocked it back.

Taking a deep breath, she looked up at him, still standing in front of her. "I've lost *everything*. What do I do now?"

Shane sat beside her and took her hands in his. "You take a breath. You're a strong, resilient woman, and you've suffered a tremendous blow, but I have no doubt you'll recover." Her hands were warm, but she was still trembling. "Why don't you take a shower and then see if you can sleep for a bit?"

"I don't even have any clothes."

"I'll lend you a T-shirt, and when you wake up—if you want me to—I'll help you figure out the rest."

Shane led her to the shower and was waiting when she stepped out. He gently dried her then slipped one of his shirts over her head. "Do you want me to dry your hair?"

"You have a hair dryer?" For the first time, Norah managed a faint smile.

"With this hair?" He chuckled. "Of course I do."

There was a bench near the soaker tub, and she sat on it to let Shane dry her hair. When he finished, he led her into the hall and hesitated. She looked at him, waiting.

"I'm not sure where you'll be more comfortable, my room or the guest room," he said.

She shrugged. "I can't even think."

Shane led her to a corner room with glass on two sides. He pushed a button, and blackout shades silently descended. Norah pulled back the duvet and climbed between the most luxurious sheets she'd ever felt. Shane put an extra blanket on top of her then left.

Several hours later, she woke up and went looking for Shane. At the top of the stairs, she heard voices. *Is that Caitlin?* She walked down and found her friend talking to him. Bags surrounded them.

Cait saw Norah and enveloped her in a hug. "Sam called to tell me what happened. I went shopping for clothes for you and Piper. When I stopped at Sam's, he gave me Shane's address." She had tears in her eyes. "Norah, I can't believe what you went through. I'm so glad you and Pip are okay."

235

"How is she?"

"A little weepy, but she told me all about it."

"I need to see her, to touch her. This is like a terrible night-mare." She looked at Shane.

"Sam called while you were asleep, and they're coming over," he said. "Piper wants to see you as much as you want to see her."

After Caitlin left, Norah opened the bags. "I can't believe she did this." She pulled out leggings and a top. "It's handy to have a friend who knows your size and style."

"That's a good friend." Shane took her hand. "Are you feeling warmer?" When she nodded, he said, "You have many people who care about you. Ava stopped by." He pointed at the couch, where there were more bags. "She brought you some clothes too."

"How did she find out? God, I hadn't even thought about work. I'm a mess."

"You're entitled to be a mess. Sam called her. He's called everyone he can think of to let them know what happened." He grinned at her. "Including your mother. She called an hour ago."

Norah rolled her eyes. "How did she know your number?"

"I gave it to Sam last night, along with my address. She wants to know that you're okay. When you're ready, you should call her."

While he was talking, Norah saw Sam drive in. He'd bare-ly stopped the car when the door was flung open and Piper

236

hopped out. She ran toward the house, and Shane opened the door wide. Norah stepped out and scooped her daughter up.

"Mommy! I dreamed that the water washed you away."

"I'm here, Pip. I'm here. We're both okay." They clung to each other for several minutes until Piper squirmed.

"Shane lives here? And Gibbs?" The dog came outside, and Piper hugged him. "Shane saved us, Gibbs. He's a hero."

Sam and Sophie joined them, and Sam shook Shane's hand. "I didn't get a chance to say it last night, but I'm grateful from the bottom of my heart for what you did. Pip is right—you truly are a hero."

Shane shrugged off the compliment. "It was a team effort. It's what Swift Water Rescue is all about."

"We went shopping, Mommy. We bought clothes for you."

By the time Pip and Sam left, it was late afternoon. As twilight gathered, lights came on in the house. Norah looked around, confused.

"They're motion activated, so they automatically turn off when not needed," he said. "I incorporated as many energy-saving features as possible when I designed the house. Would you like a tour?" When she nodded, he showed her the open concept on the first floor, where the windows went from the floor to the ceiling. "It's high-performance glass, designed to minimize heat loss and maximize natural light. The wood is bamboo, and the steel is all reclaimed. There are solar panels on the roof, and

I have a system for collecting rainwater." He stopped. "I don't imagine you want to talk about rainwater right now."

"No. But I'm very impressed. You take commitment to the environment even more seriously than I'd figured out from our conversations."

"I take it very seriously. Let's go upstairs." He showed her his room, and they walked by a closed door.

"What's in there?"

"My office."

"Where you do this and that?" Norah's curiosity about what Shane did for work was even stronger now that she'd seen the lavishness of his house.

Lavish *isn't the right word. It's simple, but everything is top-shelf.*

"Yup." He grinned but didn't elaborate.

Norah admired the clean lines, which she'd missed in the morning. "I like those shades."

"When I stayed at your house, I know you noticed that I have some sleep issues. It's not unusual for me to stay awake until early morning and then sleep late, so I need to shut out the daylight." They walked back downstairs. "How are you feeling?"

"Overwhelmed—so overwhelmed." They sat on the couch. "I wouldn't mind a shot of that bourbon you gave me last night. Actually, it was this morning, wasn't it?"

Shane poured her a glass of bourbon. She swallowed it the same way she had earlier. Then she looked around the room, which was scattered with the bags her friends had dropped off.

"I've lost literally everything I own, but I have the things that matter. Piper is okay, and I have friends who dropped everything for me." She leaned against Shane. "What's next? I don't even know where to start."

Before Shane could answer, headlights shone through the glass. "That's one of my team. Let me see what he wants." He hurried out the door and came back, carrying Norah's cell phone. "They found this on the floor of the inflatable."

"I thought I must have dropped it somewhere." As soon as she punched in her security code, the phone sprang to life with text messages and voicemails. She read a couple of messages, placed the phone in her lap, and wept. "So many people who care." Shane stretched his arm across her shoulders, and she leaned against him. "I can't read all these right now. Do you think it's okay if I don't respond until tomorrow?"

"That will be fine." He stroked her cheek.

Falling asleep didn't come easily, and after she dozed off, nightmares of standing in the rain with Piper and watching the floodwater tear her house from its foundation roused her repeatedly. Each time she woke up, gasping for air, Shane was there, holding her, comforting her. She finally fell into a deeper, dreamless sleep and awoke to Shane standing beside the bed, holding a mahogany tray laden with a plate and two mugs of coffee.

"You didn't eat anything yesterday. I made you some breakfast." He set the tray down, picked one of the mugs off it, and sat in a nearby chair. The plate held an omelet, several sausage links, and pieces of fruit.

She struggled to swallow a bite of the omelet then put the fork down. "It's good."

Shane watched her. "*Good* would be you gobbling it up."

She stabbed a piece of fruit and brought it to her mouth. "I don't feel very hungry." She choked the fruit down. "Did you sleep with me?"

He nodded. "I heard you wake up a couple of times, and I came in to comfort you. I decided it would be easier if I stayed here. I hope you don't mind." As she picked at the food, he said, "Sam called earlier to see how you are. Piper is going back to school tomorrow."

Norah's face crumpled. "I feel like she should be with me."

"Sam said she's having the same trouble sleeping that you are. He and Sophie have her in bed with them." He reached for her hand. "I'm not telling you what to do, but maybe a couple more nights to get your emotions under control would be good."

"I know you're right." Tears filled her eyes. "I don't have a house. How am I going to have her with me? I'm lost. Where do I even start? I sound like a broken record."

"You start at the beginning. I'd like you to stay here. You can have this room, or you can sleep with me. I know you don't want to be separated from Piper, and she's welcome here too." He took a deep breath. "You're going to hate me. I discussed it with Sam. I'm a bit far away for school days, so we talked about him having her during the week and you having her on the weekends. He said you did something similar when he was hurt but in reverse. I know it's none of my business—"

"Stop. I'm completely overwhelmed. I can't do this on my own." Norah started to cry.

Shane moved from the chair to the bed and held her as she wept.

"Damn it. I'm not a crier. I hate this," she said.

"Hon, you've been through a major, major traumatic event. You're allowed to cry."

Chapter Twenty-Five

Picking Up the Pieces

Norah

THREE DAYS LATER, SHANE parked his truck at the end of what was left of Norah's driveway. She climbed out of the truck, and he took her hand as they walked to the deep crevasse where her house had stood. He'd tried to talk her out of coming here, but she'd insisted. The night before, she'd woken only once from the nightmare, and she'd finally started eating more. They stood at the edge of the gully, looking down at the once-again-peaceful stream.

The storm had washed away the two houses south of Norah's, and their owners were climbing over the rocks, searching for anything salvageable. Shane and Norah climbed down the bank, picking up and discarding things as they walked. The air was still, in stark contrast to the noise of Sunday night. A patch of blue caught Norah's eyes, and she knelt to find a sodden clump of material. She pulled it apart then dropped it, drawing in a sharp breath. She stood up and started back toward the truck, trembling. Shane was closer to the river, and he scrambled to reach her. He wrapped his arms around her as she shook the same way she had after the rescue.

She pointed toward the discarded clump of cloth. "That's our Christmas pajamas from last year." She buried her head in his shoulder. "You were right. I can't be here."

Sam dropped Piper off that afternoon, and she clung to Norah, not squirming to be put down like she usually did. He told her that Piper hadn't woken up with nightmares the past two nights but hadn't gone back to her own bed either. Norah said they were going to put her to bed in Shane's guest room and hope for the best.

That night, Norah stayed with her until she fell asleep then joined Shane in the living room. A shot of bourbon had become their evening ritual, and he had one waiting for her. She curled up in an overstuffed chair.

"You need to think about a car. I know you don't want to depend on me—or anyone else." The day before, he'd helped her start a list of things she needed to do and guided her to the local, state, and federal agencies that might offer assistance.

"All the things that we went over yesterday—how do you know all that? I work for a state agency, and I had no idea who to reach out to. I'm sure I could have figured it out, but you made it so much easier."

"Someone close to me lost their house in a wildfire in California. I helped them navigate putting their life back together." He walked to the bar and held the bottle out. "Another?"

"No. I will not let this turn me into an alcoholic."

Shane raised his eyebrows. "I don't see you ever succumbing to any kind of addiction. I told Gibbs early on that you were the most tight-assed woman I'd ever met." He grinned. "I may have used a word other than *woman*."

"You called me a bitch, didn't you?" Norah was grateful to be feeling playful with him. "You wouldn't be the first. And I was bitchy to you when we first met." She grinned back at him. "But you talked to your dog about me? I'm not sure how I feel about that."

"Gibbs and I had several long conversations about you."

"Can I come over there?" Norah pointed at the couch.

"You know you don't have to ask."

She rose from the chair and settled next to him. "Did you get my text—the one I sent when I was driving home from Connecticut?"

"I did. And then I blocked your number." Shane rubbed her shoulder. "I was angry at you for not inviting me, and I was angry at myself for caring. I figured the text was driven by horniness, and as much as I appreciated your desire, it didn't alleviate my anger. And I figured the next time Mommy and Daddy beckoned, I'd be cast aside. Again."

"Wow. I appreciate your honesty, but I feel incredibly shallow."

"You're not shallow at all. That's the problem. You're intriguing. I've wondered every day since then if I did the right thing. You didn't give me a chance to show you I'm more than a tattooed plumber."

"I stood at the party, wishing you were with me and realizing what a huge mistake I made by not inviting you. I know there's much more to you than your appearance would suggest." She smiled. "I can be as persistent as you. Are you going to accept my apology?"

"Yes. I'll accept your apology. But—"

Norah put her finger over his lips. "Cait's been telling me for years that I need to break free from my parents' expectations. I'm not perfect, and I'll probably backslide, but the life I want is here in Vermont. At least, that's what I decided while I was standing alone in that ballroom in Connecticut. Now I don't know what my life is."

"Will you stay with me and let me help you figure it out?"

"I'd like that. I don't want to do this by myself. Is it hard going through this again, watching someone rebuild their life?"

Shane twirled the glass in his hand. "I don't want a sympathy relationship."

"My God." Norah's eyes opened wide. "Was it you? You lost everything in a fire?"

"No. It was my parents. I was an observer, and my siblings and I helped them regroup. I don't want you to feel sorry for me or them. We're all fine." He kissed her hair. "We've got to get you some more of that jasmine-scented shampoo." He stood, extended his hand to pull her up, and hugged her. "And eventually you'll be fine too."

They looked in on Piper, asleep in the guest room. "Are you going to sleep with me? We'll leave the door open. Are you okay with her knowing that I'm more than a friend with a dog? I *am* more than a friend, right? That's what our conversation..."

"Yes. You're more than a friend."

Norah awoke a few hours later, and Shane's side of the bed was empty. She put on the robe Caitlin had purchased for her and checked on Piper, who was sound asleep, clutching her unicorn. The door to his study was open, and the lights were on. Shane was sitting behind a desk, typing on a laptop. He was wearing glasses, and Norah watched as his eyes went back and forth between a notepad and the keyboard. He finally looked up, grinning when he saw her.

"Are you working on this or that?" she asked.

"It's *this* tonight." He chuckled. "Come in and sit down." He motioned toward the chair in front of the desk.

"Will I disturb you?"

"I'd love to have you here. I have some things I need to share with you, and this is the best place to do it."

She approached slowly, trying to absorb everything in the room. She sensed that this was a much more personal space than the others she'd seen. Pictures of Shane adorned one wall. She recognized his father in a few of them and knew the others in the photos must be his siblings and his mother. Norah smiled at one of him and Gibbs in the kayak. Floor-to-ceiling shelves filled with books stood behind his desk. She curled up in the chair, tucking the blanket around her legs.

"Do you have one of these on every chair?" Norah looked toward the couch in front of the window and saw a similar blanket, neatly folded, on one of the cushions.

"Yes." He watched her study the room.

"They're very soft. Cashmere?"

"Yes. I'm not into having a lot of possessions, but I buy what I like, and I like quality."

247

She focused on the bookcase, trying to read the titles, curious about where his reading tastes went, beyond the passion they shared for Hilton Shaw. The books were too far away for her to make out, and she was too comfortable to get up and move closer. *Besides, he invited me to sit here. He didn't invite me to come and see what he's working on. What the...?*

"Is that an Emmy?" Her eyes were resting on a statuette near the top of the shelves. "Actually, are there two of them?"

"Yes."

"Are they yours?"

He smiled. "Yes. Just as the Rolex is real, those are my Emmys."

Her eyes narrowed, and she studied him. "You're not an actor, are you?"

"No. I was a screenwriter—a very successful screenwriter until I broke a colleague's jaw."

"When you were twenty-eight. That's what knocked you down a peg?"

He nodded ruefully.

"Is that what you're doing now—writing a screenplay?"

"Actually, it is. For the first time in twelve years." He came out from behind the desk, rolling his desk chair. He stopped in front of Norah and sat facing her. "I should have told you this before now."

Shane gave her a brief version of his life story, describing how he'd fallen apart after his success and then found his passion for writing again at Bread Loaf.

"I'm an author." He took her hands. "I didn't tell you because in my prior life, people fawned over me because of what I did and what they thought I could do for them. Believing that hype about myself turned me into an asshole. I swore that would never happen again. If someone didn't like me as a simple plumber, I didn't want them in my life. None of the people I count as close friends know that I'm a writer. A successful writer."

"You write under a pen name?"

"Yes. I adopted a pen name because I didn't want my novels to be tainted by my former reputation. You could have found out all about Shane Hilliker, the douchebag, if you'd googled me.

"It never occurred to me you might be someone famous. I'm sorry. Would I know anything you've written?"

"If you didn't suspect I was famous, it means I've done my job well. Don't be sorry." He walked to the bookcase, pulled out a book, and walked back. He handed it to Norah and sat down, watching her intently.

She studied the book title then looked up at Shane. "You're Hilton Shaw?"

He nodded.

Norah looked repeatedly between Shane and the book. She opened it, thumbed through the pages, then placed it in her lap. "It all makes sense. Your books reflect your concern for the environment and climate change. It was right there in front of me." She shook her head. "Wow. This is a lot. I've lost everything and found out I'm..."

She was going to tell him she was in love with him. *I can't do that. My emotions are all over the place.* "I don't know what to say."

Shane walked back to the bookshelves, selected another book, and handed it to Norah.

"Married to Mystery? I haven't read any in this series, but Ava raves about it." She pointed at him. "You?"

He nodded. "I'm Hildy Shackleford."

Norah burst into laughter, and Shane joined her. "I mean, you are as far from a twenty-seven-year-old female as I can imagine." The laughter felt good. "Is there anyone else?" She was still chuckling.

"No. I struggled after leaving you that note, because you'd been transparent with me. You told me about getting your tubes tied. That's got to be one of your deepest, darkest secrets."

She interrupted him. "*The* deepest and darkest."

"And you trusted me with it. I hid an enormous part of myself from you. I feel guilty about that."

"Your reasons are legitimate. I'm gobsmacked. I've been having sex with Hilton Shaw."

Shane grasped her hands and brought her to him. "Hilton hopes we get to do that again. He enjoyed making love to you."

Before she fell asleep that night, Norah murmured, "I've lost everything, and I'm sleeping with Hilton Shaw. What kind of universe is this?"

The next day, she walked into the kitchen while Piper was watching *Paw Patrol*, with Gibbs curled by her side, and Shane was talking on the phone. Norah listened to his side of the conversation from the doorway.

"She didn't wake up once. She slept in my bed. Uh-huh. So, it's okay for her to crawl in with us? I'll have pajama pants on." Shane burst into laughter. "Yeah, okay. Thanks for calling." He turned and saw Norah. "That was Sam. He called to see how the night went for Piper."

"Did you tell him about your sleeping attire?"

Shane shrugged. "He said he didn't mind if Piper crawled in with us, and I wanted him to know I'd be properly clothed."

"Oh my God." Norah covered her mouth and shook her head. "First, I find out you're a famous author, and now you are casually chitchatting with my ex. The world's gone mad, and I've lost all control."

Shane gently tugged on her hand and leaned down to kiss her.

"I like control," she said.

"I figured that out."

A week later, Norah returned to work but found herself unable to focus. Every article she read stirred memories of standing in the pounding rain with the water rising around her. She tried to dive into the project she'd been working on before the flood, and all she could think about was her house being ripped off its foundation. After two weeks, she found herself reevaluating her plan to go back to work.

"I'm thinking about taking a six-month sabbatical," she said one night, lying in Shane's arms.

Shane squeezed her shoulder. "Thank God."

She separated from him, turning onto her side, and propped her head on her hand. "What does that mean?"

"I've watched you suffering, but I know you have to work it out on your own, so I haven't said anything."

"A colleague from Natural Resources approached me today. Ava asked him to talk to me because she recognized my turmoil. He suggested a sabbatical and was sure it would be granted." She took a deep breath. "Shane, I've never not worked and not had my own income. That's important to me."

"It's important that you take the time to deal with every-thing." He stroked her hair. "I've lived alone here for over three years, and I love it, but having you here, it finally feels like home. I want you here, and don't care if you have an income or not. I know you don't want to depend on anyone, but please, let me take care of you, at least for a little while."

The sabbatical was approved a week later. Shortly later, Shane came home from a meeting with Marcia to find Norah at the counter in the kitchen, furiously writing in a notebook while looking at the screen of the laptop he'd purchased for her. He approached her from behind and kissed the top of her head. She jumped and turned to face him.

"I didn't mean to startle you," he said.

Her face was flushed. "Are you aware the storm that washed away my house was the fourth one like that in Vermont this year and that there was a similar storm in Connecticut two months ago? These storms come up with little warning and cause millions of dollars in damage in tiny areas."

The storm that had destroyed her house affected less than one square mile but had dumped eight inches of rain in less than three hours.

"You're excited. Good excitement?" he asked.

"That's hard to say. I'm horrified to read about the devastation, but I think I've figured out what I want to do. I'm going to immerse myself in researching these storms. They must be a direct effect of climate change. I had a call today from James Collins. He's a climatologist and has a small lab in the southern part of the state. He asked me to join it. But I don't think that's for me. I want to tell my story. I'm going to make it personal. There needs to be a face for the damage we're doing to the planet, and I'm going to make it mine."

Shane set up a desk for her in his study, and she enjoyed having him nearby to bounce ideas off. She spoke with scientists leading the study on climate change as well as municipal and state officials from around the world who were rebuilding after storms comparable to hers, or more severe. Early one afternoon, Norah ended a call, shaking her head and muttering to herself.

He took her hand. "Come on. We both need a break. Put on some warm clothes." The sun was shining, an unusual occurrence for late November, but the air was chilly.

She came back wearing fleece-lined leggings that Shane had encouraged her to buy, along with a heavy sweatshirt. Wrapping her arms around him, she asked, "Where are we going?"

"I have a spot I want to show you before snow flies." He slid his hands down her hips and ran them over her butt. "Have I told you lately how much I enjoy having you here?"

"Only every day."

They walked often, but Shane had not taken her to the spot at the height of his property. "This is beautiful." Norah looked in every direction, finally settling her gaze on the Connecticut River to the east. "I'll confess, I don't want to be any closer to a river than this."

"Understandable." Shane sank into the chair and pulled Norah down into his lap. "I've put snowshoes for you and Piper in my LL Bean cart so we can come up here in the winter. Is that okay?" He checked in with her on every purchase.

Norah nodded her approval and could see how that pleased him.

"I'll put another chair up here in the spring. It's one of my favorite places to come and clear my head." He nuzzled her neck and hair and inhaled. "This is where Isolde came to life."

"You know she's my favorite character." Norah had read the screenplay.

"I modeled her after you."

"What?" Norah turned so she could see his face.

"I was having a hard time getting started after leaving you, because every bit of the story made me think of you. I told Marcia I wanted to make Dai female, but that spark was quickly extinguished."

"Come on. Dai couldn't be female. Everyone loves him."

Shane nodded, chagrined. "I know, but you were everywhere. I came up here and decided to give Isolde a stronger role, and that you would be my muse. It unlocked the door, and I was able to start writing."

"I'm not sure what to say. Thank you?" She kissed him.

"I'm glad she's your favorite. I envisioned a character everyone would want to be. Fierce, independent, dedicated to her cause. I know I'm on the right track, and watching you since the flood has made writing her even easier." He smoothed her hair, his fingers bumping against one of her ears. "You're cold. We should head back." They stood for a few minutes, looking out over the valley. Shane grasped her hands and gazed into her eyes. "I love you. I won't do something dumb like ask you to marry me, but I hope you'll be with me for a very long time."

"I want that too. You're showing me I can let myself be vulnerable and you won't take advantage of that. I love you, and I want to see what kind of life we can build together."

Six weeks later, Norah started a Substack entitled *Our Fading World*. Within a month, she had amassed a large following and was invited to be interviewed on several podcasts. In May, one year after meeting Shane, she had her first speaking engagement.

"Good afternoon. My name is Norah Taylor, and I'm a victim of climate change."

The End

Epilogue

Shane

SHANE TAPPED HIS TOE nervously as he sat in the greenroom, waiting for his appearance on *Entertainment Tonight*. "Go bravely in the direction of your dreams." Marcia had left this quote from Henry David Thoreau, the day after they returned from the first trip to Hollywood. And now, his dreams were on the brink of coming true. Along with dreams he hadn't even known existed. With ten minutes to go, he Face Timed Norah. "Hey, Hon."

He could see Piper on the couch next to her, wrapped in a purple cashmere blanket. His color palette had run to shades of gray before Norah moved in, but when he found out Piper's favorite color was purple, he'd ordered several of his favorite blanket in shades of purple ranging from light lavender to deep mulberry. He liked the color that Norah and Piper had brought to his life.

"Mom and I watched you on *The View*. I can't wait to see you on *Entertainment Tonight*. Are you nervous?"

Norah had become *Mom* shortly after Piper turned nine. Shane and Norah suspected it had as much to do with Sam and Sophie giving her a little brother as it did with growing up. And in two months, Sophie was expecting a little girl. Piper was beyond excited that she'd be getting a sister.

"Not too nervous. I enjoy talking about the movie."

"Yeah, like Mom likes to talk about us almost getting washed away." She snickered. "Winnie's puppies are almost ready to go." Sam and Sophie had gotten a golden retriever soon after Norah moved in with Shane, and she'd had puppies six weeks earlier. "I have the one I want all picked out. Gibbs is looking forward to having a friend."

Shane and Norah hadn't agreed on the puppy yet. But he knew they would.

Piper's resilience amazed him. Norah had been slower to heal, but her new endeavor had provided the last piece. She'd traveled all over the country, telling her story, and she had summer speaking engagements scheduled for Europe. Shane and Piper would go with her, and they would spend a week exploring Italy when she was done with her work.

"Marcia called today. She's had an inquiry from China." Norah smiled at him. "Do you already know?"

"No." Shane said firmly. When Marcia had signed on as Norah's agent, the three of them had agreed that Norah's and Shane's businesses were to be kept separate. "China, huh?"

"I told her I'd need to schedule other presentations in Asia. It makes little sense to travel all that way for one presentation."

"I agree with that." There was a knock on the greenroom door. "I think they're ready for me. Love you guys." He winked at Norah and headed toward the stage.

Standing in the wings, Shane heard the host introduce him. "Our last guest for the evening is Shane Hilliker, the screenwriter for *Beneath the Burning Sky*, one of the most highly anticipated movies of this season." Shane strode onto the stage and shook the host's hand. "Welcome, Shane. It's good to have you here."

"I'm glad to be here."

"Let's dive right in. How did you get this coveted gig? I know you worked as a television screenwriter, but that was several years ago. This is a big movie. It seems like they would have wanted a bigger name."

"You're very direct. I like that. My environmental concern was well-known during my time in Hollywood, and I worked with Steve Jensen on my first job. Steve is the driving force behind the movie. Talking Hilton Shaw into allowing the movie to be made was no small feat, and he was adamant that the screenwriter share his fears about climate change. So Steve thought of me, and the timing was right. I'm excited to be part of this."

"Did you get to meet Hilton Shaw?" the host asked.

"I did. We spent a day together discussing the direction I was going in with the script."

"All of America is dying to know. What's he like?"

"He's a charming man who has serious and legitimate concerns about the effects of climate change. He hopes his writing will raise awareness, but he has no desire to be part of the story."

"Will he attend the premiere?"

"No, he likes his quiet life and doesn't want to be a part of that scene," Shane said.

"I know I speak for the fans of *Beneath the Burning Sky* when I say I can't wait for the premiere. I appreciate you taking the time to talk to us today."

"Thank you. I think the movie will please everyone."

Three days later, Shane gazed into the mirror and slipped the knot of his tie into place, thinking back to his trip here more than two years before. He smiled as he remembered how he'd stopped at Norah's on his drive home and ended up in her bed. She brought more joy to his life than he'd thought possible. He wished she was with him, but one of her speaking engagements conflicted. His tie was a gift from Norah. Made from organic hemp, it featured a leafy design and complemented his olive-green shirt, also hemp. As Norah rebuilt her wardrobe after the flood, she worked diligently to buy clothes made from sustainable fabrics. Shane had joined her effort, enjoying the way their interests meshed.

Shrugging on his blazer, he made his way to Marcia's room. She would be his date for the premiere, and they would walk the red carpet together.

Shane smiled as he stood in the doorway to the bathroom in his room at the Beverly Hills Hotel. Norah was immersed in bubbles, with her eyes closed and earbuds in place. They'd been in California for almost a week while he did press prior to the Academy Awards ceremony, which would be the next night. The success of *Burning Sky* was overwhelming, and Shane had already received a Golden Globe and an award from the Writers Guild of America. Marcia was inundated with offers for Shane, but he was determined not to become enmeshed in Hollywood culture again. Talks for a sequel to *Beneath the Burning Sky* were already underway, and the producers wanted Shane.

He shook his head, then lightly touched Norah's shoulder. She started, and her eyes popped open. He leaned down to kiss her.

"Hey, beautiful, sorry I was gone for so long."

"I was fine. Who wouldn't be in a place like this?" She stood, and Shane snatched a towel to dry her. He fluttered kisses from her earlobe down her neck to her breast. His tongue teased the nub.

Norah sighed. "Don't we have dinner plans with your family?"

Shane groaned as he straightened up. "You're too damn practical."

"Just one of the things you love about me." Norah smiled as she danced away from him. "Let me get ready." She reached her hand to his chest and dragged it down to the bulge in his pants. "I'll be looking forward to time on the balcony with you throughout our dinner." They'd been ending their nights with a glass of wine on the balcony before Shane carried her to bed.

"That balcony was where I decided to put more effort into wooing you. It was one of my better decisions."

"Are you ready for the insanity?" he asked. They were riding in a limousine, and this would be Norah's first time to walk the red carpet with Shane.

"I can't wait to see you receive the recognition you deserve."

"It's not a guarantee. All the screenwriters nominated are talented and wrote great scripts. I refuse to take anything for granted."

The limo stopped, and the driver hopped out to open the door. There were crowds of boisterous fans hoping to catch a glimpse of their favorite performer. Shane was happy they were looking for movie stars and didn't care about screenwriters so he and Norah could proceed to the carpet in relative obscurity, but he knew the television hosts showcasing the arrivals would buttonhole them, and he couldn't wait to share that spotlight with Norah.

"Approaching us now is Shane Hilliker, the screenwriter for *Beneath the Burning Sky*. He's been cleaning up this award season and is the frontrunner tonight. Shane, thanks for taking a minute to chat with us."

"Always happy to talk to you, Shawna."

"Hope you have your speech ready, because the buzz on the street is that an Oscar is coming your way."

"We never know how the Academy is going to go, so I'm not taking anything for granted." He fingered the notes in his pocket.

"Always humble. Tell us what you and your lovely companion are wearing tonight."

"I'm happy to do that. This is Norah Taylor, and in keeping with our environmental and sustainability concerns, we shopped at Curated Classics in Beverly Hills. My tuxedo is vintage Pierre Cardin, and Norah's dress is vintage Ralph Lauren. My necktie, gold to match Norah's dress, is made from organic hemp."

"Very befitting for your movie. Good luck tonight, Shane."

He slid his arm around Norah's waist. "Whew, we survived that."

"You're smooth with the press. Our friends in Vermont will be impressed."

They walked down the aisle and sat in the fifth row, with Norah on Shane's left and Marcia on his right. He gripped Norah's hand throughout the show, trying to quiet his nerves. *Burning Sky* won for film editing, production design, visual effects, and best supporting actress. In her speech, the winner thanked Shane for creating the character of Isolde.

He leaned over and whispered in Norah's ear. "All because of you, hon."

Finally, the show reached the writing awards. "The Academy Award for best adapted screenplay goes to..." The presenter paused for what seemed like hours while tearing open the envelope. "Shane Hilliker for *Beneath the Burning Sky!*"

The theater erupted in applause as Shane turned to kiss Norah. He stood, hugged Marcia, and made his way to the stage. He accepted the Oscar and lifted it high in the air.

"Wow!" His smile was broad as he reached into his pocket. "I have some notes because that's what writers do. First, thank you to the Academy. This is a great honor. Next, I'm grateful to Steve and the other producers. They took a chance on me when I hadn't written a screenplay in several years, and I think it turned out okay. To all the actors involved, you made my words sing. Thank you. My family, thank you for keeping me grounded and not letting me forget my roots. And finally, to my partner, Norah Taylor, thank you for being a bright light. Since Norah and her daughter, Piper, came into my life, I'm more dedicated to the battle for our environment than ever, and I will forever be grateful to Hilton Shaw for giving that fight a voice. Thank you all."

Afterword

Did you enjoy this book? If you did, leaving a review on Amazon or Goodreads is a wonderful way to let the author know. Reviews are one of the most powerful tools in an author's arsenal.

Sneak Peak

JENNY

Jenny reached for Robbie when she awoke but found his side of the bed empty. She lay quietly for several minutes, thinking about their lovemaking the night before. The memory of it made her clit throb again. It had always been like that with him. When they met, she'd been twenty-four and had ended a long-term relationship six months earlier. Jenny had been with other guys on a more casual basis, so she wasn't inexperienced, but from the first time Robbie made love to her, she felt like she was being introduced to a whole new world.

Robbie walked in with two steaming cups of coffee, and she scrambled to a sitting position to take one.

He crawled into the bed and gently kissed her. "Good morning."

She loved reconnecting on the weekend. "Good morning to you. How are you feeling?" They'd both consumed a lot of alcohol during the game and at O'Malley's. She was shocked she didn't feel hungover.

"Not too bad. Bit of a headache when I got up. It was that damn shot of Jameson that Caden and Danny insisted on."

She shook her head as she grinned at him. "Peer pressure gets you every time. You should know better."

"I know. I know. How about you?"

"Surprisingly, I feel fine."

"It must have been that superior sex when we got home." He took a sip of his coffee.

"Superior, huh?"

"Are you going to tell me it wasn't?"

"No, it was outstanding." She paused. "It's been a while since we've gone at it with that much abandon." She frowned. "And I know that's probably on me. My focus has been on the timing and..."

He put his finger on her lips. "Stop. We both want a baby, so we've both been concerned about doing it at the best time in the optimal position. It's not your fault." He moved his finger away from her mouth. "But if the heat generated last night has any effect on conception, then we've surely got quintuplets on the way."

They laughed, and she said, "If only it worked that way."

Robbie had his arm over her shoulders, and he stroked her hair. "What's on your agenda for today? I hate to do this, but I had an email this morning that one of my guardian ad litem kids got moved to a new foster home yesterday. I kinda want to go check on him. Would you mind? I'd be gone an hour or two at the most."

"Of course I don't mind. We both know how much those kids need you." She turned and kissed him. "I've got all the regular stuff to do to get ready for the week. We'll go for our walk when you get home? They tried to go for a long walk every Sunday.

"Absolutely! Let's have some breakfast, then I'll head out."

After Robbie left, Jenny got in the shower and, as the water cascaded over her, she smiled thinking about his involvement with the guardian ad litem program. Eight years earlier, he had walked into the neighborhood center where she was doing an internship as the final piece of her graduate program. She was weeks away from getting her master's degree in social work and trying to decide whether to stay in Boston or return to Minnesota, where her family lived.

Robbie had been dressed in a T-shirt and dark-wash jeans that hugged his narrow hips and long legs. His blond hair was longer than how he currently wore it, and Jenny thought he looked like he should be carrying a surfboard. His blue eyes collided with her green ones, and she felt a tingle as he looked her up and down.

Before he could say a word, she asked, "Did you take a wrong turn on the way to California?"

"Uh, California? Why would I be going to California?"

She detected a slight Southern accent. "Aren't you looking for a beach to surf on?"

"No." He looked confused. "Can y'all tell me where to find the director's office?"

"What do you want with the director?"

"My professor told me to talk to her about volunteering."

"Your professor?" After spending the entire semester at the center, she was used to the steady stream of college students looking for a spot to work to pad their resumes. They came dressed in their career-advancing best clothes, and most of them only lasted a week or two. The inner city was not for the faint of heart. "What college are you from?"

"Harvard Law School." His look challenged her to come back at him.

"You don't look like a lawyer."

"Well, I'm not quite there yet. One more year of law school. Would I be more acceptable if I were dressed in a suit and tie, darlin'?"

Jenny blushed.

He continued, "I thought the kids might be more comfortable with a more casual attire. Now, the director's office?"

"Down this hallway, second door on the right." As he started walking, she called after him, "Don't turn left. You'll end up on a California beach, and you forgot your surfboard."

He stopped for a second, started to turn around, then raised his arm with a wave instead.

She had watched him until he reached the director's open door.

Jenny stepped out of the shower, smiling at the memory. *He was so sure of himself. And I was so smitten.* As she dried her hair, she thought more about that day.

She had been almost ready to leave when he finally walked out of the director's office. He'd been with her much longer than most prospective volunteers, and she heard laughter, which was unusual. He headed directly for the door, and she wondered about his abrupt departure, disappointed that he hadn't stopped to talk to her on his way out.

A couple of minutes later, as she was closing her laptop, the door opened, and when she looked up, he was walking back in.

He stopped in front of her desk. "Do you live nearby?"

She narrowed her eyes and asked warily, "Why?"

"I wondered about the parking situation. Do you drive here?"

"I don't drive anywhere in the city! You actually want to drive your car?"

"I need to get to my job across town at the end of the day, and I'm not sure the T will get me there in time. Having my car would make it easier."

"Sorry, can't help. I use the T or a ride share. How often will you be here?"

He grinned. "Three days a week. Serving as an advocate and mentor for the kids. The director liked my T-shirt."

She sputtered. "I didn't *not* like your shirt. You just aren't dressed like most people who come in looking to volunteer."

"You'll find out I'm not like most people, darlin'." And with that, he turned to leave again. He stopped at the door. "Would you like to get something to eat?" Her wariness showed, and he said, "I saw how you deflected my question about where you live. I might be a serial rapist, and you don't want me to be able to track you down."

She continued to look at him with hesitation in her eyes.

"That was wise. I'm glad you watch out for yourself, but I assure you I'm harmless. I really did just want to know about the parking situation, but now... I'd like to get to know you." He walked back to her desk and extended his hand. "Rob Hatch."

"Jennifer Hagen. We don't want to eat around here. It's not the best neighborhood."

"Suggest a destination. I'm open to anything."

She was jittery, still hesitant.

"The blue line will get us to my neighborhood, and there are lots of fine restaurants there. I'll get you a rideshare to take you home after we eat. Send your two best girlfriends a text that you're getting a bite to eat with this incredibly handsome surfer you met today. Let them know you'll text the name of the restaurant in thirty minutes." His eyes twinkled at her.

"Are you always this persistent?"

"No."

She did what he suggested, texting her roommate and her best friend. They walked to the T stop, and he told her where they would get off. She smiled because it was the stop she took to get to her apartment. He suggested a pub she'd been to many times. As they walked in, the hostess greeted them by name.

After they sat down, Robbie asked, "You've been here before?"

"I have. My apartment is nearby."

He raised a hand. "Stop. Don't tell me where. Not till you know me better."

She laughed. "Do you live close by?"

"I do. But I'm not telling you where because I'm not sure that you aren't a serial axe murderer."

She rolled her eyes.

"Are you going to text your friends to let them know where we are?"

"If I do that, they'll come here to check you out."

"I'm not scared. I'll check out okay."

"Cocky much?"

"I prefer to think of it as self-confident."

"Where'd the Southern accent come from?"

"I lived in Tennessee from three to fourteen, then my family moved up here. I fell in love with Boston and stayed when they moved to the Pacific Northwest two weeks into my senior year."

"Where'd you live?"

"A friend's family took me in. We went to Boston University together. Now, he's in med school and I'm in law school. We share an apartment. So I'm not cocky, but I've been on my own for quite a few years, and I am sure of myself. I'm not hearing any Boston in your accent. Where's home?"

"Minnesota. I'm just finishing up my master's degree at Simmons."

"What's next?"

"I honestly wish I knew. I'm done in two weeks, and my apartment lease is up at the end of June. I'm trying to decide whether to stay here or go home."

Her hand was resting on the table, and as he gazed into her eyes, he put his hand on top of it. "You should stay here. I'm looking forward to working with you at the center. Mrs. Smith said you've been working as a mentor and advocate, just like I will be. I think we'd make a dynamite team."

"What brought you to the center? There are dozens of places you could volunteer that would be more convenient and more relevant to a law career."

"You, darlin'. You led me there."

"Oh my God." She laughed.

"I've got this pathological need to give back." He shrugged. "I have no idea where it comes from."

Jenny put her hair dryer down. *And with that, I fell in love with him.*

Follow Jenny and Rob's struggle to have a child and catch up with what happened to Quinn and Caden on their return to Boston in *Whispers of Hope* coming September 18, 2025

Author's Note

A<small>T THE SAME TIME</small> that I was plotting Norah's story, I was starting to look into Climate Fiction as a genre I wanted to include in my writing. I learned that it could vary from dystopian Science Fiction works to literary fiction developed hand in hand with climate scientists.

From the very first time I wrote about Norah, she has been a climate activist and when I decided to explore her story, I knew her environmental concerns would be a factor.

In July of 2024, my town and the surrounding area was hit with two devastating flash floods, less than three weeks apart. There were lives lost, and tremendous damage to public and private property. The storm that swept away Norah's house was modeled after those floods.

I've watched my town struggle to rebuild infrastructure, and seen businesses make significant investments to repair and re-open. My friends and neighbors are wrestling with whether to stay on their property or walk away, and I've realized that climate fiction does not have to be dystopian. It is here with us every day and while my desire is always to write love stories that entertain, with this book I wanted to share our storm story and pay tribute to the many individuals affected by it.

Also by

Whispers of Goodbye
Whispers of Forgiveness
Whispers of Mistletoe
Whispers of Starlight
Whispers of Healing
Whispers of Change

About the author

SUE IS AN AVID reader who ventured into the writing world during the first year of the Pandemic. Her stories showcase men and women working to become whole and happy. Family plays a prominent role as do the steamy encounters which come with falling in love.

Sue is a lifelong Vermonter who counts books, sunsets, and travel as vital to her being. Mountains, from the slopes of Vermont's Greens to the towering peaks of Colorado's Rockies feed her soul.

Her children are grown and flown and she's living her happily ever after with the boy she met in a college library fifty years ago.

Follow her on Facebook, Sue Mills – Author

Or on her website, suemillsauthor.com

Or on Instagram, suemillsauthor

SUE MILLS

And TikTok, Sue Mills, Author

280